LIARS

4

Viper is one
step ahead...

For all the readers who helped me get to book #30!—Jack Heath

Scholastic Australia
An imprint of Scholastic Australia Pty Limited
PO Box 579 Gosford NSW 2250
ABN 11 000 614 577
www.scholastic.com.au

Part of the Scholastic Group
Sydney • Auckland • New York • Toronto • London • Mexico City
New Delhi • Hong Kong • Buenos Aires • Puerto Rico

Published by Scholastic Australia in 2019.

NATIONAL LIBRARY OF AUSTRALIA
A catalogue record for this book is available from the National Library of Australia

ISBN: 978-1-74299-342-3

Typeset in Versailles LT.

Printed in China by Hang Tai Printing Company Limited.

This product is made of material from well-managed FSC®-certified forests, recycled material, and other controlled sources.

FSC www.fsc.org MIX Paper | Supporting responsible forestry FSC® C023121

10 9 8 7 6 5 4 3 2 1 25 26 27 28 29 / 2

LIARS

4

LOCKDOWN

JACK HEATH

A Scholastic Australia Book

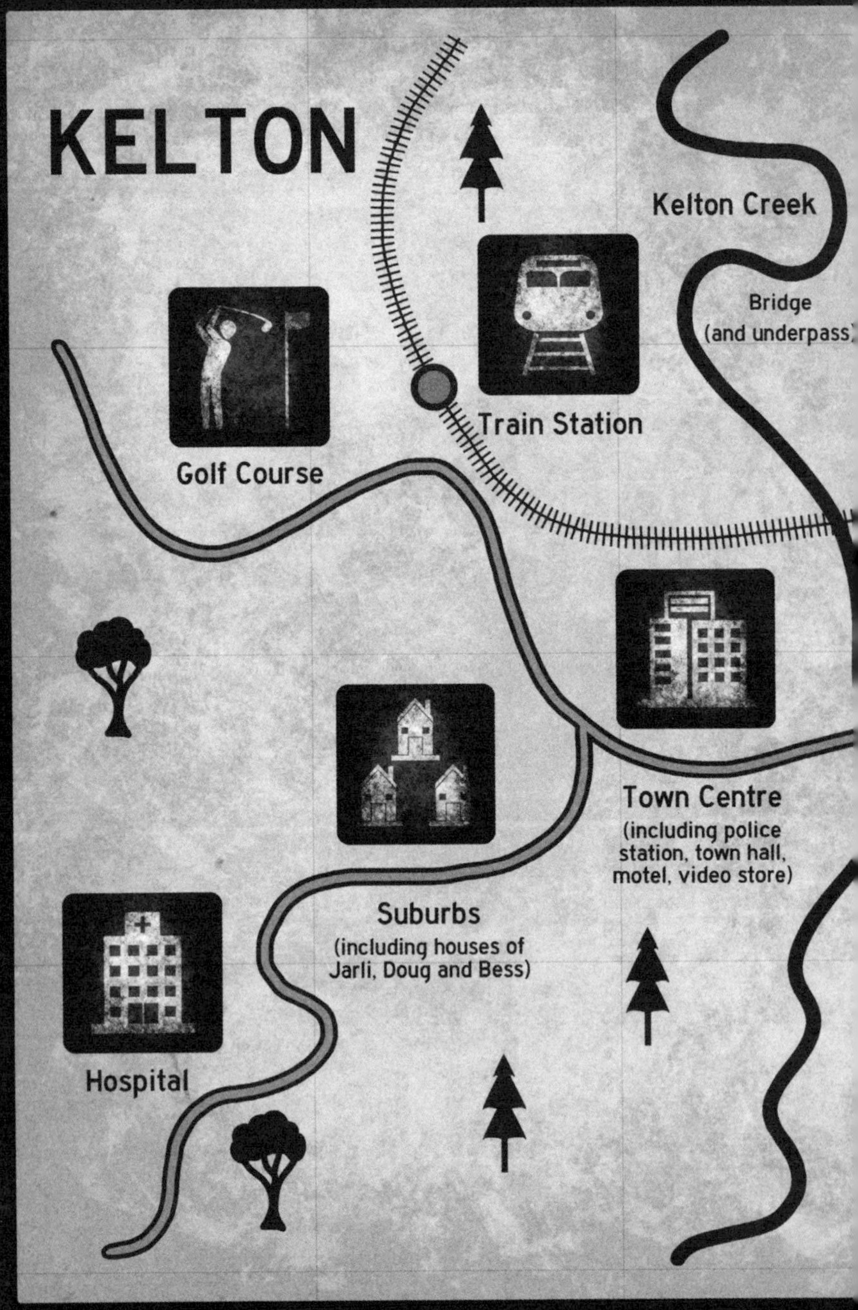
KELTON
Kelton Creek
Bridge
(and underpass)
Train Station
Golf Course
Town Centre
(including police station, town hall, motel, video store)
Suburbs
(including houses of Jarli, Doug and Bess)
Hospital

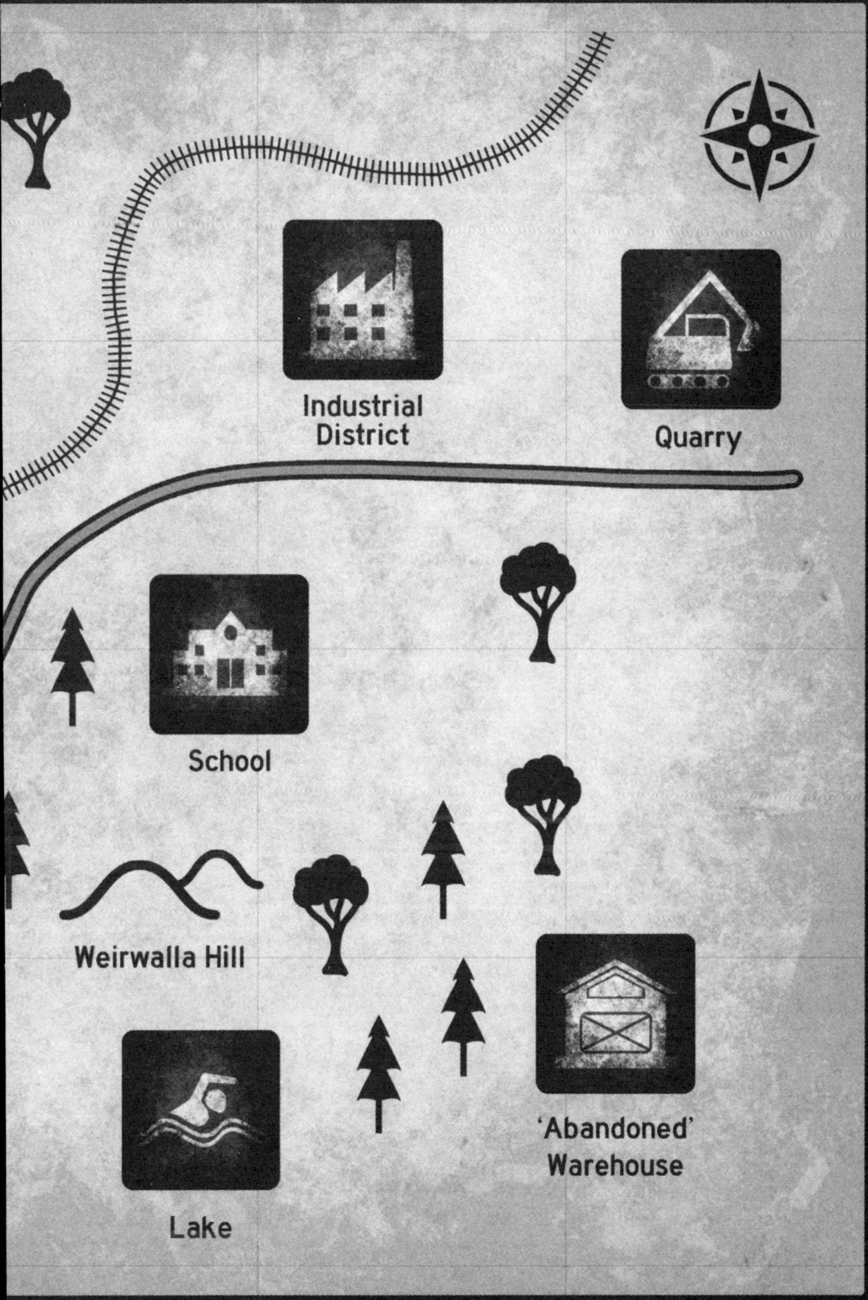
Industrial District
Quarry
School
Weirwalla Hill
'Abandoned' Warehouse
Lake

PART ONE: EMERGENCY

'JUST BECAUSE YOU HAVEN'T HEARD SOMEONE LIE, THAT DOESN'T MEAN THEY'RE HONEST. YOU NEED TO HEAR THEM TELL THE TRUTH WHEN THEY WOULD HAVE BEEN BETTER OFF LYING. IT'S NOT UNTIL THEY OFFEND SOMEONE OR CONFESS SOMETHING THAT YOU CAN TRUST THEM.'

—*From the documentation for* Truth, *version 4.1*

LEAVE A MESSAGE

REPORT 091

UNDERCOVER AGENT: COBRA
COVERT SURVEILLANCE OF TARGET D03

TRUTH_PREMIUM***START_TRANSCRIPTION//

>Pick up the phone, Jarli.
>Pick up the phone!
>Listen, it's Kellin. Can you hear me? I know who Viper is. And that's a very dangerous thing to know. Viper has already made dozens of people disappear. I don't want to be next.
>I can't go to the police. Absolutely anyone could be part of Viper's network. You're the only one I trust. Please, please, pick up!
>I've hidden the evidence somewhere safe. Even if Viper finds it, the data can't be erased. But I don't know how I'll—
>Hang on.
>Someone's at the door.

//END_TRANSCRIPTION***TRUTH_PREMIUM

ACTION: VIPER ALERTED
THREAT: NEUTRALISED

DEADLIEST SUBSTANCE IN THE WORLD

'What's in there?' Jarli asked, pointing.

The steel door had four big, electronic locks. Through triple-layered glass, Jarli could see two people in airtight hazmat suits stacking plastic crates on shelves. The cold left a mist in the air and fogged the window.

'Hazardous samples,' Dr Lanagan said. She was a small, bony woman with bright red glasses, and grey hair tied back so tightly it stretched the skin of her scalp. 'Now, if you'll all follow me—'

Some of the students started to follow her, but Jarli was still curious. 'Samples of what?'

Lanagan shrugged. 'Various things. If we take something out of a patient's body that might be contagious, toxic or radioactive, we store it in there.'

'Why not destroy it?' asked Anya, an athletic girl with angular features and a faint Russian accent. Jarli thought she sounded suspicious of Lanagan, but he could have been imagining things. She was hard to read.

'There's an incinerator in the basement,' Lanagan said. 'But the samples need to be studied first. Sometimes we keep a disease for years, hoping to develop a cure. Hence the security.'

'So there are incurable diseases in there?' Doug asked. A lanky boy with blond hair, Doug had seemed sullen and hostile when Jarli first met him, and Jarli had eventually found out that Doug's family was in witness protection. Now he and Jarli were friends, sharing a passion for tech. They had volunteered for the science excursion hoping to check out the surgical robots.

'Kids,' Mr Hayes said. 'We came here to learn about the brain.' He was starting to look uncomfortable. He was a PE teacher, called in to replace Mrs Prive at the last minute, and he may have been out of his depth. He was even wearing his exercise shorts and polo shirt, which didn't suit the cool air of Kelton Research Hospital.

'Take botulism H, for example,' Lanagan said, ignoring the teacher. 'It's a toxin made by the botulina bacteria, and it's the deadliest substance in the world. A millionth of a gram could kill everyone in this room by slowly paralysing our bodies, including our hearts and lungs. A litre jug of it would be enough to make the human race extinct.'

The kids stared at her, horrified. Even Mr Hayes

looked shaken. For a moment the only sound was the rain, drumming on the hospital roof.

Lanagan smiled faintly. 'You can see why we lock the door. Now, who wants to see a human brain?'

'Me!' Bess stuck up her hand eagerly. Bess was Jarli's best friend—a girl with a half-shaved head and a perpetually cheery attitude. If anyone could shrug off a speech about the extinction of humanity, it was her.

'Right this way,' Lanagan said.

This time everyone followed. Hayes looked relieved. As they walked away, Jarli took one last peek through the glass. The people in hazmat suits had finished stacking crates and had entered an airlock full of high-pressure hoses. Water sprayed their suits from all sides. He hoped they were being careful.

Lanagan had a long stride for a short woman. Bess was on crutches, but she managed to keep up. 'How many patients get brain surgery here per day?' she asked the doctor.

'Zero, usually.'

'How many per week?'

'This is primarily a research hospital. Most procedures are performed at the regional public hospital.' Lanagan shot Jarli a look. 'The only patients we have here are those in need of emergency care.'

Jarli's cheeks grew hot. He'd been taken to the ER twice this year. In February he and his father had been in a car crash. In May he had nearly drowned in liquid nitrogen after breaking into a factory owned by reclusive billionaire KELLIN PLOWMAN.

None of this was Jarli's fault—he had been targeted by a mysterious criminal mastermind known only as Viper. But it sounded like the hospital staff saw Jarli as a nuisance.

Lanagan walked past the sign to **SURGICAL THEATRE 2,** and pushed open a pair of double doors leading to **SURGICAL THEATRE 1.** The students followed her in. Racks of stainless steel blades were mounted above big sinks. A stereo system was built into the wall on the opposite side. Blue cloths were draped over several tables. Stalk lamps hovered over tables, like at a fancy library. An MRI machine took up most of one corner. There was a window, but because of the storm clouds outside, it didn't let in much light.

A huge mechanical arm towered in one corner. A surgical robot.

Doug made a beeline for the robot. Jarli should have been excited, but he felt suddenly uneasy. He remembered a statistic he'd heard somewhere: *one in four people who enter a hospital will die there.*

He hoped this stat didn't include kids on school

excursions. It probably came from big city hospitals with busy emergency rooms. The Kelton hospital was quiet—he hadn't seen a single patient since he arrived.

'Why do you need all this equipment if you hardly ever use it?' Doug was asking.

'We do use it—for research,' Lanagan replied. 'Take a look at this.'

She swivelled one of the stalk lights around, illuminating a glass container. As the light fell across the object inside, Jarli gasped.

'Left over from a previous experiment,' Lanagan said. 'Ordinarily we would keep body parts in the morgue, but the morgue is closed until we can replace the flammable cladding in the walls.'

'What *is* it?' someone asked.

'A slice of brain matter, less than a millimetre thick. The tissue surrounded a brain tumour—we removed it from the subject, put the sample on ice and took it downstairs to the lab, so it was still alive when it arrived.'

The piece of brain looked like a branch of coral. The light shone right through the yellow-grey flesh—it looked as fragile as tissue paper.

'Still alive?' Hayes said incredulously. 'Outside of the patient's head?'

'Indeed. It's dead now, but for a while we could

actually see the neurons firing—sending signals back and forth. And that's important, because your thoughts and feelings and memories are not made of neurons. They are made of the *connections* between those neurons, which are only visible when they fire.'

Jarli wasn't sure if it was the surgical tools or the brain slice, but he was beginning to feel nauseous. He hoped the excursion would move on soon.

Bess peered through the glass. 'Are you saying this slice of brain was *thinking?*'

'Probably not,' Lanagan said. 'Conscious thoughts make up very little of a brain's activity. Most of the time it's just telling your heart to beat, your stomach to keep digesting, and doing other things you can't control. But we're working to identify patterns of connectivity across the entire brain. Someday this will help us to remove faulty neurons, treating neurological diseases with increased precision.'

'What did the connections in this piece do?'

'We're still sifting through the data, but we think they processed information from the inner ear. The patient woke up with severe vertigo, and couldn't stand. Don't touch that!'

Doug stepped away from a device that looked a bit like a handheld barcode scanner, mounted on a trolley. 'I was just looking,' he said.

'That's one of our laser scalpels,' Lanagan told him. 'It's designed to vaporise soft tissue. And you, young man, are made mostly of soft tissue.'

Doug took another step back.

To Jarli, the walls felt too close, the ceiling too low. He wasn't even sure of the way out—the hospital was a maze. He stuck up his hand. 'Can I go to the bathroom?'

'Me too,' Anya said quickly.

Hayes sighed. 'Does anyone *else* need to go to the bathroom?'

Thanks to his tone, no-one else owned up.

'Alright,' Hayes said. 'You two, go. But come back quickly.'

'The closest one is near reception,' Lanagan said, pointing. 'Out the door, turn left, and then down the stairs.'

Jarli pushed through the double doors. As soon as he was out of sight, he took a deep gulp of chlorine-scented air and stretched his arms out wide, fighting off the claustrophobia.

Anya came out through the doors. She nudged Jarli. 'You OK?'

'Yeah. Just needed some air.'

They started walking along the corridor towards the stairs. Alcohol-based hand-sanitisers were mounted on the walls outside every room. The floor had been polished so many times the colour had worn off the tiles.

'So,' Anya said quietly. 'What did you want to talk about?'

Jarli looked blankly at her. He had assumed she honestly needed to go to the bathroom. He didn't need to talk. He had just wanted to get out of there.

'You sent me a message a few days ago,' Anya prompted. 'You said you had something to tell me.'

'I did?'

Anya snorted. 'It must not have been very important.'

'Sorry,' Jarli said.

'Don't be. I am relieved. I thought it might have been something to do with . . .' She made a snake-like motion with her hand. It took Jarli a moment to realise she was talking about Viper.

Jarli wasn't the only one who had been targeted by the mysterious criminal. Cobra, one of Viper's men, had kidnapped Anya soon after ramming Jarli's car. Viper had also crashed a plane into Doug's house, and been involved in an attempt to kill a prominent politician. The worst part was, no-one knew exactly what Viper wanted. Money? Political power? Or something else?

Maybe Anya was too scared to say his name out loud. Jarli felt the same way.

'No,' he said. 'I haven't heard anything.'

'It's been two months since he tried to kill the defence minister. The police must be getting close.'

'Must be.'

Jarli's phone beeped. LIE It had been scanning his words for signs that he wasn't telling the truth.

Anya heard the beep. 'You do not think they are?'

It was annoying, being caught out by his own app, but Jarli preferred to leave it switched on. Not just to tell him when other people lied, but to tell him when *he* did. Jarli thought of himself as an honest person, but it was amazing how many small lies the app caught him telling each day, mostly because the truth was rude. He would say, 'I have to get going,' instead of 'I don't feel like talking to you right now.' Or he'd say, 'I appreciate your help,' instead of 'I wanted to do that myself.' When his sister asked if he liked her haircut, he'd say 'Yes,' instead of 'You look like a cockatoo.'

'Vi—the man they're looking for,' Jarli said. 'He has advanced tech, heaps of money and spies everywhere. He's willing to murder people to keep his identity a secret. I don't think the police will ever find him.' He shivered. 'Come on—we'd better find the bathroom.'

They both walked down the stairs. Jarli could hear an ambulance siren getting louder and louder.

'Maybe you are being a bit cynical,' Anya said. 'The police might have some good luck.'

'They might. But how good has our luck been lately?'

Just as they reached reception, the front doors slid open, and a disaster came in.

BLOOD LOSS

Two paramedics ran into reception, pushing a wheeled stretcher. Jarli couldn't see much of the patient—he was wrapped in a blanket, and a breathing mask was strapped to his face. But he could see the splotches of blood on the sheets. Something very bad had happened to him.

Jarli recognised one of the paramedics, a man with sideburns and a mop of orange hair—Tyson. He was the same guy who had come to the scene of Dad's car crash, and had showed up again when a plane ploughed into Doug's house. Kelton had a small population, so the same faces showed up a lot. Jarli hadn't met the female paramedic before.

'BP's at eighty-six over forty-eight,' she was shouting. 'His heart rate's dropping. Forty beats per minute.'

Jarli and Anya stared, aghast. A doctor and a nurse ran up to the gurney. Jarli knew both of them—Dr Vorham and Nurse Amon. Vorham was tall, with silvery hair and a gaunt face. He had taken an interest in Jarli when he arrived in the ER covered in liquid nitrogen burns, and he had been helping Jarli's father, whose facial scars weren't healing properly since the crash. Amon was smaller, with a beak nose and watchful eyes. He wore navy blue scrubs—Jarli wondered if the dark colour was to hide bloodstains.

'What do we have?' Vorham asked.

'Multiple contusions and fractures,' said Tyson. 'A bone fragment might have nicked the femoral artery.'

'Do we know what happened to him?'

'The police found him in a car crusher,' the female paramedic said. She was a pale woman with thin eyebrows and dark plaited hair.

Vorham didn't seem surprised to hear this. 'Tell Dr Lanagan to scrub up for surgery,' he said.

'She's with a school group,' Amon said.

'Get them out of the way, ASAP,' Vorham said. 'This will be hard enough without a bunch of kids looking over my shoulder.'

Vorham and Amon took the gurney and pushed it through another set of doors towards the lift. Tyson ran over to the reception desk and snatched up the phone.

'Code blue. Dr Lanagan to scrub up for surgery in Theatre One.' His voice echoed over the PA system throughout the hospital. 'Lanagan to Theatre One. Code blue.'

'She's already there,' Jarli said quietly.

The female paramedic noticed Jarli and Anya standing nearby, looking shell-shocked.

'Hey,' she said. 'Jarli, right? I'm Olivia. We met yesterday.'

'We did?' Jarli was too shaken to remember anything from more than five seconds ago, but he was pretty sure he had never seen Olivia before.

'A van dropped you off in front of the video store,' she said. 'You looked lost. I asked if you were OK.'

Jarli didn't think any of that had happened, but his app didn't go off, so the paramedic believed what she was saying. She must have seen him on TV—the app had made him briefly famous—and then met someone else who looked like him.

'Will that man be alright?' Anya asked.

'He's in good hands,' Olivia said.

If Jarli's phone had been running *Truth Premium*—a rip-off of his own app, *Truth*—it probably would have told him that Olivia was reframing. But he didn't need an app to notice that Olivia had avoided answering Anya's question.

Jarli had uninstalled *Truth Premium* when he discovered it was created by Viper. The master criminal had hijacked the publicity around Jarli's app and used it to market his own version. Viper's app was more sophisticated than Jarli's, but it had a secret feature—a whitelist. There were certain people the app always trusted, no matter what they said.

'Did you say he was in a car crusher!?' Anya was asking.

Olivia nodded. 'Police were investigating a break-in at the scrap yard, and they heard screaming from inside the crusher. They switched the machine off as soon as they could, but . . .'

Jarli shuddered. He had seen the crusher at the scrap yard, and heard the shriek of tortured metal as it worked. The thought of being trapped inside would give him nightmares.

'Did the injured man work at the scrap yard?' Anya asked.

Olivia coughed. 'Uh, no. That was Kellin Plowman on the gurney. He—'

'Kellin Plowman?' Jarli exclaimed.

Plowman was the eccentric billionaire who owned the factory Jarli had been burned in. Later, when they met in person, Plowman had offered to buy Jarli's newest creation, a homemade firewall.

He had made his fortune by inventing a new kind of encryption. Jarli had once tried to break it, just for fun. Like all the tens of thousands of nerds before him, he had failed.

Plowman was the one who had told Jarli that *Truth Premium* was made by Viper. And now he'd been found in a car crusher. Jarli felt sick.

'Did he say who did this to him?' Anya asked.

Olivia hesitated, perhaps realising that she shouldn't be talking about a patient to two random schoolchildren. 'You kids should find your teacher. Sounds like you'll be getting back on the bus pretty soon.' She turned away to talk to Tyson.

'I can't believe it,' Jarli whispered to Anya. 'I just talked to him last week.'

'What about?

'Uh . . .' Jarli tried to remember. 'I was asking him a question about Supply Chain.'

'What is that?' Anya asked.

'Plowman invented it. It's a sort of de-centralised ledger,where information is shared across thousands of different servers and devices, but protected by a cryptographic hash function so no-one can modify—'

'You have already lost me.'

'The point is, it's a really good way of keeping secrets,' Jarli said. 'And I got the feeling Plowman knew something he wasn't telling me. About Viper.'

They were interrupted by a squeal of static. Tyson was fiddling with the radio on his hip.

'What was that?' Olivia asked.

'Not sure. Maybe the batteries.'

Olivia tried her own radio. It made the same shrieking sound. She flinched and turned down the volume.

'Must be a faulty broadcaster somewhere on the network,' she said.

Tyson looked up at the ceiling. 'Great. That's all we need. Come on—we'd better get back out there.'

Just as the automatic doors started to open, something flew through the gap and skittered across the floor. It looked a bit like a soft-drink can, but smaller. Jarli peered down at it, noting that there was no brand name. Just black metal.

'Close your eyes!' Anya yelled.

Jarli was too slow. A brilliant light FLASHED out of the can, dazzling him. There was a tremendous *bang*—a wall of noise which left him reeling. Blind and deaf, he staggered backwards until he hit the wall. He reached out, trying to stop himself from falling over, but he couldn't find anything to hold onto. Soon he was on the floor, too stunned to even cry out.

EMERGENCY SURGERY

'CODE BLUE. DR LANAGAN TO SCRUB UP FOR SURGERY IN THEATRE ONE. LANAGAN TO THEATRE ONE. CODE BLUE.'

Bess wasn't sure what a code blue was, but it sounded like an emergency.

Lanagan didn't panic, though. 'I'm afraid you'll all have to leave,' she said. 'Right now.'

She strode over to a button on the wall marked **STERILISE.** When she pushed it, the air filter started roaring overhead, sucking contaminated air out of the room and pumping clean air back in. Lanagan hurried over to a huge industrial sink and started washing her hands.

Mr Hayes didn't need to be told twice. 'Come on, kids,' he said, ushering them towards the door.

Bess lingered. 'What's going on? What's a code blue?'

'It could mean a lot of things,' Lanagan said. 'None of them good.'

Hayes herded Bess out of the surgical theatre after the other students. He let the doors fall closed behind him, silencing the noise from the taps inside. There was a faint sucking sound as the rubber seals connected—the theatre was airtight.

'Well, then,' Hayes said. 'That's life in a hospital, I suppose. Come on, everyone—back on the bus.'

'Early mark?' someone said hopefully.

'*Maybe*. Depends when we get back to school. We may have time for a quick maths lesson.'

Bess groaned. A faint smile hovered on Hayes' lips. He was messing with them.

As the group walked back, a pair of lift doors slid open up the other end of the corridor. A doctor and a nurse rolled a stretcher out. A man was strapped to it—pale, limp and bleeding.

'BP's fallen to eighty-two over fifty-five,' the doctor was saying. Bess recognised him—Dr Vorham. He was a specialist in movement disorders. Her parents took her to see him once per year. But this patient looked like he was in need of much more urgent attention.

'Kellin?' the nurse said. 'We need you to stay awake, OK?'

The patient's groan was little more than a phlegmy rattle.

Kellin? Bess's eyes widened. She tried to connect the battered face of the man on the stretcher to the face she had seen at Jarli's robot battle, but he looked completely different.

'Make way!' the doctor cried. He and the nurse were pushing the stretcher dangerously fast. Anyone standing in the way, would be flattened. As the stretcher passed the students, Bess saw that one of the man's arms was bent at an ugly angle, as though he had too many elbows.

'Mr Plowman,' Bess whispered.

One of Plowman's eyes was concealed behind a bandage. The other, bloodshot, fixed on Bess. 'Tell him . . .' he whispered.

His voice was muffled by the mask. Bess strained to hear over the rain drumming on the roof.

'Will . . .'

'Who is Will?' Bess reached for his hand, but the doctor and the nurse were still pushing, and the stretcher was already out of reach.

'Compound fractures in these two ribs,' the nurse was saying. 'And I'm worried about his spine.'

'Looks like arterial bleeding from his thigh,' Vorham said. 'If we don't deal with that, it won't matter what we do about his spine. Do we know his blood type?'

'Not yet. Test takes ten minutes.'

'This man doesn't have ten minutes. There's some universal donor in the theatre. Lanagan can start transfusing that while I stop the bleeding.'

Vorham took control of the stretcher and pushed it into Surgical Theatre One. He called back to the nurse, 'Once you have the test results, bring us more blood in his type.'

'On it.' Ignoring the students, the nurse ran past towards the stairs.

Bess and the other kids stared in horror as the double doors to the theatre closed and the wounded man disappeared.

What happened to him? Bess wondered. *Did he fall off a roof? Get hit by a truck?*

She clutched her crutches a little more tightly. When she was a child, she'd tumbled headfirst out of a treehouse. The accident had left her unable to walk normally, or to control the occasional spasms in her muscles. These symptoms hadn't been obvious until the rest of her body healed. With Plowman's body so wrecked, it was hard not to imagine what damage might be hidden beneath the surface.

Panicked babbling filled the air. The kids up against the wall were jostling, trying to see if the stretcher was gone, while the kids up the front were trying to back away from the trail of blood droplets on the floor.

'Students,' Hayes bellowed. 'Calm down, please. We're going to head back to the bus. When we're all back at school, we'll talk more about what just happened, and I'll call the hospital to check that the patient is OK.'

That seemed unlikely to Bess. The guy had been a wreck.

'They called him Kellin,' Doug whispered. 'Do you think it was . . .'

'You'd know better than me,' Bess said. Doug had met Plowman at the Robattle, and Doug's mother had once worked for Magnotech, a company Plowman owned. When Viper tried to buy an electromagnetic weapon from Magnotech, Doug's mother had contacted the police. Viper had responded by using the weapon to crash a plane into Doug's house.

Before today, Bess had only ever seen Plowman in the distance. He owned a fancy golf resort at the edge of the town. He didn't like golf, but he used the green to test out drones. Bess had sometimes seen quadcopters circling the area, and a man in a broad-brimmed hat holding a remote control.

'I guess it kind of looked like him,' Doug said, looking shell-shocked.

Bess cringed. How would she break the news to Jarli? He and Plowman were friends, sort of.

'Poor guy,' she said. 'You reckon someone tried to rob him, or what?'

'Back to the bus, everyone,' Hayes was saying. 'Follow me.'

They were still twenty or thirty metres from the lift when the doors opened again . . .

And a man with a grenade walked out.

SNAKE PIT

Jarli looked around. His eyes were still adjusting. The world was a mess of washed-out shapes. He could see people moving, but he couldn't tell which ones were Anya and Olivia.

And there was something huge. The size of a rhino or a minivan, swooshing across his field of blurry vision. As soon as he blinked, it was gone.

We're under attack, he thought. But there was nothing he could do about it. He couldn't even stand up. The noise had messed up his balance. Vertigo—like someone had tampered with his brain.

A strange thought popped into his head: *How did Anya know it was a flash grenade?* It had just looked like a soft-drink can.

The ringing in Jarli's ears started to fade, and soon he could hear voices. At first it was like listening to a foreign language. The words meant nothing. But then his brain recovered enough to decode the sounds.

'Room one clear!'

'Four civilians neutralised.'

'Doors secure.'

'Rattler, kill the phones. Anaconda, go seal the back exit.'

Someone grabbed Jarli's shoulders and shook him like a rag doll. He tried to fight the person off, but it felt like his arms were made of spaghetti.

The hands let go of him. 'I figure we have about fifteen minutes before this one's up and about,' a voice said.

'Plenty of time. How about the others?'

'Paramedics are immobilised. The girl's unconscious. Turn on the jammer.'

'I already did.'

'Are the phones down?'

'Yep. No calls in or out.'

'OK. Taipan, Mamba, you two find the target.'

Jarli blinked furiously, trying to clear the fog from his eyes. He found himself looking at Anya, who was slumped on the floor with a puddle of drool under her mouth. Maybe she'd hit her head on the way down.

'Anya,' Jarli said. It came out like 'Nah'. His tongue felt floppy.

She didn't react, but someone else did. A tall woman with broad shoulders and a leather jacket approached Jarli. She was carrying a big sword—

a cutlass, like the kind a pirate might use.

'You're awake,' she said. She had an American accent. Her voice was hard, like a VILLAIN from a video game. 'Can you hear me?'

Jarli tried to nod, but his head wouldn't move. He blinked instead.

'OK,' the woman said. 'Here's the deal. We've sealed the hospital. We've cut off all communications. No-one can leave, and no help is coming. But if you do as we say, nobody will get hurt. Got that?'

Jarli's phone beeped. LIE

DO NO HARM

The man Bess saw coming out of the elevator had a short, military-style haircut and swim goggles over his eyes. He was tossing the grenade from one gloved hand to the other like a cricket ball, and whistling between crooked teeth. Under his black coat, two ammunition belts crossed his chest.

It was a moment before anybody reacted. Bess had enough time to think, *Who wears swim goggles inside?* And then: *Crikey, that looks like a grenade.* And then: *That* is *a grenade!*

She grabbed Doug, who'd been ambling next to her, oblivious. 'Are you seeing this?' she whispered.

Doug froze. His eyes widened in alarm. One of the other kids saw the man and screamed.

The sound made Hayes turn around. 'What the . . . everyone get back! The other way, quick!'

'What's up?' someone demanded from the back of the group.

'Go that way, towards the stairs!' Hayes told the students. 'Hurry!'

'Why?'

'Just do it!' As the grenadier approached, Hayes pulled a red handle on the wall—a fire alarm. A harsh *BEEP, BEEP, BEEP* filled the corridor. The grenadier ignored the noise, smiling as he strolled towards them.

The class fled the other way towards the stairwell. Bess fell behind immediately. Her crutches made it hard to run, and it was worse when she was stressed. Her heart hammered her ribs as she limped after the other kids.

When she risked a look back, she saw that the squat man was following them at a brisk walk. Slower than all the other students, but faster than Bess. He would catch up to her soon. The fear felt like a live animal in her chest.

Doug noticed that Bess had fallen behind. He ran back and grabbed her arm.

'Lean on me,' he hissed.

Bess wrapped her arm around his shoulders. He carried one of her crutches as they hobbled towards the stairs, like in a three-legged race. Faster than the grenadier. But he didn't look worried that the kids were getting away. He moved like he had all the time in the world.

'Can you make it to the bottom of the stairs?' Doug asked.

'Yes.' *Pretty quickly, if I fall,* Bess thought. It had happened before.

And then someone screamed up ahead.

'Turn around!' Hayes yelled. 'Back to the room!'

As the kids at the front of the group turned, mouths gaping, faces drained of colour, Bess saw what they had seen. Someone else had emerged from the stairwell. A woman with a vineyard of tattoos on her bare arms, boots which came up to her knees . . . and a crossbow. She looked like a vampire slayer.

Now the corridor was blocked at both ends. The teacher and students were trapped between a grenade and a crossbow. There was no way out. But maybe they could barricade themselves in one of the surgical theatres.

Everyone panicked, fleeing from the woman. In the chaos, Bess was nearly knocked over. She clung to Doug, fighting to stay upright.

'I'd advise you all to stay where you are,' the grenadier shouted from the other end of the corridor.

But Hayes was holding open the doors to Surgical Theatre 1. 'Hurry, hurry!'

The students flooded through the doorway. Doug and Bess were last. Hayes slammed the door behind them.

'What's going on?' Dr Lanagan demanded. She was wearing a smock and a surgical mask. A scalpel was in her gloved hand. Plowman lay on an operating table behind her.

Despite the fire alarm, it didn't look like the doctors had any plans to evacuate. Maybe just like at school, everyone ignored the beeping stage of the alarm. It wasn't until the second stage, when the siren wailed, that got people moving.

'Does this door lock?' Hayes asked.

'You need to leave,' Lanagan said. 'Immediately.'

'This room has to be kept sterile,' Vorham added.

'There are people with weapons outside!' Hayes shouted. 'We're under attack!'

Lanagan looked shocked. 'What people? What weapons?'

Vorham just raised an eyebrow.

Footsteps approached in the corridor outside.

Bess looked around for something heavy they could drag in front of the double doors to seal them. But all the furniture was bolted down. Instead, she jammed her crutch through the doorhandles.

Just in time. The handles rattled as someone pushed from the other side.

The doors were solid, made of thick wood. The crutch was only aluminium, but it held.

'Locked,' a voice said. The tattooed woman.

'Hello in there,' the grenadier called. His voice was oddly formal. 'I assume you can hear me.'

Everyone inside the theatre looked at one another in anxious silence. Bess realised she was holding her breath.

'Kids,' Vorham said quietly. 'I think you should move away from the door. You too, Mr Hayes.'

Bess followed as the other students scampered into the corner. But there was nowhere to hide.

'The police are on their way,' Lanagan shouted. 'They would have been notified as soon as the fire alarm went off. If I were you, I'd be gone before they get here.'

'I assure you, madam, they are not on their way. We have cut the telephone lines, and brought two frequency jammers to block any communication from mobile phones or other devices. The rest of the hospital staff and patients have been secured in the basement. The only people aware of the fire alarm are those inside this building.'

As if on cue, the beeping stopped. All the lights in the room flickered at the same moment.

'See? My colleagues and I have plenty of time,' the grenadier said.

Bess couldn't resist digging out her phone to check if he was telling the truth. No signal. They were on their own

'We mean you no harm,' the grenadier continued. 'Just give us Mr Plowman, and we'll be on our way.'

A horrified silence descended. Bess looked at Plowman, unconscious and vulnerable on the operating table.

'He needs immediate medical attention,' Lanagan said, her voice wavering.

'That's not your concern.'

'He's my patient. It *is* my concern.'

'If you do not release him peacefully, we will take him by force. Mamba, would you care to estimate the number of casualties if we were to blast our way into this room?'

The tattooed woman just grunted.

Bess could hear Doug hyperventilating on the floor nearby.

'A rough guess will do,' the man pressed. 'How many died in Malburse, when we used explosives to clear a path for our retreat? Twelve? Thirteen? Of course, there were no children there. The comparison isn't apt.'

He let that hang in the air.

The name 'Malburse' hit a tripwire in some distant corner of Bess's mind. But she couldn't remember where she'd heard it.

Vorham was whispering to Lanagan. 'We have a responsibility,' he said. 'Not just to our patient, but to these students. They are also in our care.'

Lanagan shot him a withering look. 'You really

think these kids will be safe if I open this door?'

'Safer than they'll be if a bomb goes off in the corridor.' Vorham's voice remained calm.

It's like he wants them to come in, Bess thought.

'I'm waiting,' the grenadier said.

'He's my patient,' Lanagan said loudly. 'I swore an oath.'

Bess heard the grenadier sigh. 'Is that your final answer?'

'It is.'

'History will remember you for your foolishness. For the lives you could have saved.'

'History will remember *you* as the man who blew himself up trying to break through a very strong door.' Lanagan turned back to the operating table and switched on the laser scalpel. 'Dr Vorham, get the next transfusion ready,' she ordered.

Vorham hung a bag of blood on a hook. 'It's our last one,' he warned.

'You should use the remote detonator, Taipan.' Mamba's voice was raspy, as though she was recovering from the flu.

'No. We'd have to switch off the signal jammers. Don't worry, this will work.'

Bess braced herself. She and the other students were huddled only five or six metres from the door. If the bad guys tried to blast their way in, the students would be showered with debris. Even if they weren't hurt, they had no way of protecting Plowman from Mamba and Taipan—

Bess froze. Mamba and Taipan sounded like codenames. Codenames based on SNAKES.

Viper is back, she thought.

TACTICAL UNIT MOVING IN

By the time former Constable Irena Blanco reached East Kelton, the Magnotech factory was surrounded. Two police vehicles blocked the front gates. More cop cars were parked around the back in case anyone tried to escape that way. Police snipers were visible in the windows of a three-storey office building nearby. It looked like every cop in Kelton was here. The falling rain sparkled in all the flashing lights.

A police negotiator was talking into a megaphone. 'The building is surrounded,' he said. 'Come out with your hands up.'

There was no movement from beyond the fence.

The factory had been evacuated. No smog was pouring from the smokestacks today. A safe distance away, under a temporary shelter, six workers in high-vis vests were being interrogated by Detective Zee Arno.

Blanco climbed out of her car and pulled the hood of her raincoat low over her eyes. She didn't want Arno to see her.

She walked past a row of parked cars which probably belonged to the factory workers, although one of them—a gleaming green Fiat—looked too expensive. Blanco checked the numberplate, and her worst suspicions were confirmed. Dana Reynolds, the reporter from *Nationwide,* was here somewhere. So that was two people Blanco had to avoid. Reynolds knew she had been suspended, and why.

Blanco reached the edge of the car park and walked across the muddy grass towards the nearest police car. The officer in the driver's seat was a man she didn't know. He must be new. That would explain his boring role—waiting. He would have been told to chase anyone who came through the gates. As long as none of the criminals tried to leave the factory, he had nothing to do.

Blanco rapped on the window. The officer jolted out of his trance, and rolled down the glass. 'Who are you?'

'I'm with local law enforcement,' Blanco said carefully. She didn't want to set off his lie-detector app. 'I'm not on duty right now—I just wondered what was going on.'

The officer looked doubtful until she flashed her deactivated security pass, too quickly for him to read her name. Then he puffed up his chest. 'Something big,' he said. 'But I can't talk about it right now. You'll find out all about it on your next shift.'

'I heard—' Blanco stopped herself, and rephrased: 'Is it true that there's an escaped animal in there?'

'What?' The officer shook his head. 'No. Viper is just a codename.'

Blanco breathed in sharply. So it *was* true. No wonder the entire Kelton police force had turned up. Catching the elusive crime lord had been their top priority for almost a year now.

Two days ago, Blanco had received an email from a witness. The witness claimed Kellin Plowman had told him Viper's real name. Suspiciously, the name wasn't in the email. This could mean that Viper was monitoring email communications, and the witness hadn't wanted to trigger any alerts. Or it could mean the email itself was a TRAP.

Either way, the witness had then gone dark. Blanco hadn't been able to contact him, or Plowman, to confirm this story. If Viper was here, at a factory owned by Plowman, then—

'Hey!'

Blanco turned around and saw Detective Arno storming towards her, oblivious to the rain. Her shiny black hair was plastered all over her sweaty face. She marched through the mud like a robot. A terminator.

'What are you doing here?' Arno demanded.

'Just having a look around,' Blanco said.

Arno jabbed a finger at the officer in the car. 'Did you tell her anything?'

The officer turned pale.

'Go home,' Arno told Blanco. 'Before I arrest you.'

Blanco couldn't imagine anything worse than going back to her empty duplex, watching TV and trying not to wonder what her former colleagues were up to. 'For what?' she said. 'This is a public space.'

'You're under investigation for connections to Viper. It's extremely suspicious that you're here. And if I ever find out who in this department is keeping you updated on cases—'

The officer's eyes were going wider and wider. 'Wait. You're Irena Blanco?'

'I have nothing to do with Viper,' Blanco said. 'I assume your phone is running *Truth Premium*. You can easily check that I'm not lying.'

Arno said nothing, but the look on her face told Blanco that she knew *Truth Premium* was compromised. *Interesting,* Blanco thought. Had Arno switched to Jarli Durras's original app? Or was she was sticking to the rules? It was department policy not to use open-source software.

Blanco said, 'If this is the chump you got to replace me—'

The officer frowned. 'Hey!'

'Then you're never going to catch Viper,' Blanco finished.

'I expect to have him in custody within minutes,' Arno said. 'And when I do, I look forward to hearing about all his accomplices.' With a meaningful look at Blanco, she raised her radio to her lips. 'Tactical unit one. What's your status?

Her radio crackled. 'Good to go, Detective.'

'Move in.'

'Copy that. Tactical unit moving in.'

Near the front gate, three men and two women leapt from the back of a van carrying stun guns and wearing bulletproof vests. They ran towards the factory gates, holding their heads low to keep the rain off the mirrored visors of their helmets.

'This is a bad idea,' Blanco said.

'We'll see.' Arno raised her binoculars. The tactical unit pushed through the gates and headed for the factory, running through a field of solar panels. The unit sheltered in the doorway for a moment while one of the women pressed a lock-release gun against the factory's main door. The gun whirred until the lock clunked and the door creaked open. The tactical unit disappeared inside. Blanco wondered why the door was locked, if everyone had just evacuated through it.

The radio crackled. 'Hudson, you go upstairs. Vasquez, head left, Spunkmeyer, head right. Hicks, you check out the basement. I'll take this corridor here.'

There was a chorus of *Yes, sirs,* and then silence.

'You can't even be sure Viper is in there,' Blanco told Arno.

Arno didn't take her eyes off the entrance. 'He made a phone call ordering an operative to abduct Kellin Plowman from his residence and take him to a scrap yard. We traced the call to a mobile phone, and traced the phone to this factory. According to satellite surveillance, other than the six workers who we've already identified and checked, no-one has left the building since that phone call. And before you ask, no—none of the old coal mining tunnels go anywhere near this factory. He's in there.'

'Wouldn't the solar panels interfere with the sat surveillance?' That had been a problem when Blanco investigated this factory months ago. The reflected sunshine had dazzled the satellite.

'Not in this weather,' Arno said.

'Plowman owns the factory, right?' Blanco said. 'What does Viper want with him?'

'I'll be sure to ask that when we catch him.'

'Wouldn't Viper know you can track phone calls?'

Arno said nothing. Maybe she had remembered that she shouldn't be telling Blanco any of this.

Blanco stared at the factory. Despite her sense of dread, she was excited. Maybe Viper had gotten sloppy. After all this time—all the mysterious disappearances—was it possible that they were about to catch him?

'I found something,' said a voice on the radio. 'In Section Six.'

Another voice came in. 'What is it?'

'Mystery box. Opaque plastic, a little over a cubic metre. Right under the gas pipe. You want me to open it?'

Blanco snatched the radio out of Arno's hand. 'Wait!' she said. 'Under the gas pipe is the perfect place to put a bomb.'

Arno grabbed the radio back. 'You're on suspension,' she hissed. 'You shouldn't even be here. You can't interfere with—'

'Whoa! Stop. She's right,' the radio said. 'The hinges are wired. If I open it, it'll trigger something.'

There was no time for an 'I told you so' moment. Blanco hadn't seen many bombs in her career, but she knew from her training that a demolition charge the size of a brick could bring down a building. She couldn't imagine how much damage a cubic metre of the same stuff could do.

'No sign of Viper?' Arno asked.

'None,' the voice on the radio said. 'The building's clear except for the box.'

'Then get out of there. I'm sending in Bomb Disposal.'

Arno signalled to another nearby van. Two men clambered out the back of it, their whole bodies covered in bulky armour. One of them was carrying a small robot. The bulletproof vests and helmets of the tactical unit looked flimsy by comparison, but Blanco knew that no amount of armour would save them if the bomb went off.

The five members of the tactical unit emerged from the building as the bomb disposal unit went in. Blanco couldn't see their faces through the helmets, but she was sure they were relieved. Every time she had kicked in a door with an arrest warrant, she had been terrified of getting shot, or worse, having to shoot someone else. An empty building was always a relief.

'What do they manufacture here these days?' Blanco asked.

'They recently switched from making electromagnets to making optical lattice clocks,' Arno said. 'Why?'

'If the bomb goes off, what's going to be coming

down on us?'

Arno quickly typed something into her phone. After a second, she swore and started waving her hands to get the attention of the other police officers. 'Back up, everybody! Safe distance has increased to a hundred metres.'

Blanco peered over Arno's shoulder at the phone. She could only make out a few phrases on the screen: *atomic clocks . . . strontium-87 . . . highly radioactive . . .*

Even an accidental explosion at a factory like this could be devastating. A deliberate one would be like judgement day. A rain of fire.

The police and the tactical team hustled the workers away from the factory. The snipers disappeared from the windows of the office building. Arno and Blanco climbed into the officer's car. He started the engine and drove up the road, out of debris range. Blanco felt bad for calling him a chump. He didn't seem to be panicking.

'What's your name, mate?' she asked him.

'Rodney,' he said.

'Sorry about before, Rodney,' she said.

''Sokay,' Rodney said. 'Tensions are high.'

'Detective?' It was the radio again. The bomb disposal unit this time. 'I'm looking at the hinge triggers through the robot camera. There's something funny about them.'

'Define funny, officer,' Arno snapped.

'They're glued in place rather than soldered.'

'Maybe Viper didn't have time to solder them.'

'Current doesn't flow through glue,' the man said.

'Meaning the robot can open the box?'

'There could be a real trigger on the inside of the lid. But these ones on the outside aren't connected to anything. They're fake.' He paused. 'The robot isn't dextrous enough to open the box, though. I'd have to do it.'

Arno hesitated. Blanco knew what she was thinking. Unless she gave the order, there was nothing the bomb disposal man could do. But sometimes it was easier to risk your own life than someone else's.

'Open the box,' she said finally.

The officer didn't make her repeat the order. 'Copy that.'

Blanco turned her eyes to the factory and waited for it to explode. She wanted to plug her ears, but that would have felt disrespectful to the bomb disposal men risking their lives inside. She gritted her teeth instead.

Nothing happened for a long moment. Sweat glistened on Arno's brow.

'The box is open,' the bomb disposal man said.

Blanco exhaled, dizzy with relief.

'We've got a body,' the man continued.

Arno's eyebrows shot up. 'Say again?'

'It's not a bomb. There's a person in the box . . . unconscious. Stand-by.'

'Could be Viper,' Arno said. 'Be careful.'

Why would Viper be unconscious? Blanco wondered. *Unless it's a trick. Maybe he's—*

'Oh my God,' the bomb disposal man said. 'It's Alex! Alex is in the box!'

'That's impossible,' Arno said. 'Alex is out here, with us.'

'Who's Alex?' Blanco whispered.

'The leader of the tactical unit,' Rodney replied. 'But all five of them made it out.'

'Get a paramedic in here,' the bomb disposal man replied. 'Alex is out cold.'

Arno and Blanco both turned to look at the tactical unit, who were removing their helmets. There were only four of them. One had disappeared.

Arno leapt out of the car. 'Secure the area!' she shouted. 'Don't let anybody leave!'

Blanco scanned the horizon through the car windows. There were plenty of buildings and vehicles, as well as access to the forest. Plenty of ways to escape.

It was too late. Viper—or whoever had made that phone call—was gone.

He knew we could track his phone, she thought. *He led us out here deliberately.*

Why?

INTERNAL BLEEDING

The doctors worked on Plowman, ignoring the threat from outside the door. Plowman already had so many stitches that he looked like a scarecrow. Hayes was hovering anxiously, ready to assist, but so far the doctors hadn't needed him much.

'I've stopped the femoral bleed,' Vorham was saying. 'But his BP is still low.'

'This is his second transfusion,' Lanagan said. 'You think there's internal bleeding in his abdomen?'

'Yes. We need to go in. Ramp up the pain relief.'

Bess guessed that these doctors usually had days to prepare, and more qualified assistance—someone to do the anaesthetic, someone to wipe the sweat off their brows, and probably lots of other people. And she didn't think Vorham was even a surgeon.

She spoke quietly so as not to distract them. 'Doug. You think they'll be able to keep Plowman alive?'

Doug was standing on a table, trying to open the window. 'Maybe,' he said. 'People can survive all sorts of things. There was this snowboarder who fell out of a plane without a parachute and lived. I saw it on the news.'

'Yeah, but that's *why* it was on the news. It was a freak occurrence. Plenty of people die after falling down the stairs.'

Outside, the rain had intensified. Doug gave up on the window and climbed off the table. 'It's not designed to open,' he said. 'And the glass is really thick. We're not getting out that way.'

Bess could hear the bad guys talking outside. They were speaking loudly—they wanted to be overheard.

Mamba's voice: 'How long will you put on the timer?'

'One minute,' Taipan said. 'That's the minimum. If anyone inside wants to change their mind and let us in, they don't have long to do it.'

Bess squeezed her eyes shut, and focused on the cool floor tile against her cheek.

'Wait,' Mamba said.

'What?'

'I thought of another way to get them to open the door.'

And then Bess had a thought. Something she should have wondered about much, much earlier.

Where are Jarli and Anya?

'Anya,' Jarli whispered. 'Wake up!'

Her eyelids didn't even flutter. She looked dead. Jarli cautiously pressed a finger to her neck. Her skin was warm, but he couldn't find a pulse. He might be looking in the wrong spot, though. He'd never tried this before, and he could only just reach her. His other hand was tied to a bench with a plastic cuff which bit into his wrist when he moved.

He touched his own neck, searching for a pulse.

'Relax.' The tall woman with the sword and the accent—Rattler, the others had called her—was looming over him. 'It was a flash grenade. Non-lethal. She'll be conscious in a few minutes. I'm surprised she's not awake already.'

This wasn't as comforting as she might have intended. And the sword didn't help.

As she turned, Jarli noticed something under her chin. Her face was smooth and symmetrical, but her neck was a mess of scar tissue. It looked like someone had once tried to cut her throat.

She saw Jarli looking. 'You should see the other guy,' she said with a grin. 'Hey . . . you're the kid who made the lie-detector app.'

Jarli shrank away. The *Truth* app had briefly made him a celebrity, which turned out to be horrible. He'd had to change his email address and phone number, and delete his social media profiles. His family and friends had been hassled by the media. Now it seemed that criminals had been paying attention as well.

'You must be thinking of someone else,' he said.

Rattler's phone beeped. LIE She laughed—a short, sharp bark.

'How much money did you make off that, kid?' she asked.

'I released it for free,' Jarli said quietly.

'Yeah, but you sell data about the people who use it, right?'

'No.'

Rattler raised an eyebrow. 'Really? You're an idiot.'

This wasn't the first time Jarli had faced this accusation. He didn't think being ethical was the same thing as being stupid. But he didn't want to argue about that with a cutlass-wielding criminal.

'You've interfered with Viper's plans before,' Rattler said, her grin widening. 'I can't wait to tell him you're here.'

Jarli's pulse was easy to find now. 'Anya needs a doctor,' he said. 'Maybe she hit her head on the way down.'

Rattler wiped her hands on her cargo pants

and walked back over to the window. 'Then she'll wake up with a headache,' she said. 'Like I told you, everyone will be fine . . . if they do as they're told.'

'But—'

'Shut up, Jarli,' said Olivia, the paramedic.

Jarli looked over, shocked. Olivia was cuffed to another bench, out of reach. Her voice had been too loud—maybe her ears were still recuperating after the flashbang. She was blinking furiously, perhaps trying to recover her eyesight.

'Don't antagonise them,' she continued. 'Once they have what they want, they'll leave. Then we can help Anya.'

'She might not last that long,' Jarli insisted. 'What if she has a cracked skull?'

'She doesn't,' Olivia said.

Jarli's phone didn't beep. Olivia believed what she was saying—and she was a professional. But she was further away from Anya than Jarli, and she could hardly see.

'Trust me,' she added.

Anya's chest was rising and falling, at least. Maybe she would be OK.

Lightning flashed outside the glass sliding doors. A few seconds later, thunder boomed, loud enough to shake the pens on the reception desk and the paddles of the defibrillator mounted on the wall.

Rattler didn't look up. She was fiddling with a device which looked a bit like a walkie-talkie. Jarli had heard her refer to it as a jammer. Jarli wasn't an expert—he knew software, not hardware—but he understood the basic principle. The jammer would broadcast STATIC on all wavelengths, stopping any other signals from getting through. No calls, no radio, no wi-fi, no Bluetooth. Nothing. The jammer itself could make and receive transmissions, but nothing else could.

'When will you leave?' Jarli asked. His cuffed hand was going numb.

'Soon,' Rattler replied.

'How soon?'

Rattler drew her sword. The blade caught the light from the neon bulbs buzzing above her, sending rainbows dancing across the walls.

'No more questions,' she said.

When the criminals had been talking, they had said four codenames: Rattler, Taipan, Mamba and Anaconda. Rattler was here. Anaconda had been sent to guard the back door—hopefully the school group had escaped out there first. That only left Taipan and Mamba to search the hospital for whatever they were looking for, all three storeys of it. Wouldn't that take hours? And what would happen if the school group was still here, and the bad guys found them?

'Rattler.'

A squat man in goggles was standing in the doorway. A row of flash-grenades was clipped to a sash under his jacket.

Jarli swallowed. Video games had made flash grenades seem pretty harmless. Now he knew better.

'Taipan,' Rattler said. 'What do you want?'

Taipan lifted his goggles and looked at Jarli. His pale eyes left Jarli feeling like he'd been X-rayed.

'I need to borrow a hostage,' Taipan said.

'Why?' Rattler asked.

'I require assistance opening a door.'

'Oh.' Rattler seemed to know what this meant. 'Better take two—you may need to prove you're serious.'

'An excellent suggestion. The two children should do nicely.'

'The girl's unconscious.'

'Even better.'

Rattler strode over to Jarli and swung her sword at him. The blade whipped through the air so fast he didn't have time to scream. Suddenly he could feel hot blood pouring down his hand—

No. The blood was flowing back *into* his hand. Rattler had sliced through the plastic cuff and freed his wrist without even nicking his skin.

Rattler sliced off Anya's cuff just as quickly. His heart pounding, Jarli wondered how many years of practice it took to master a sword like that—to use it as precisely as a pen. Who *were* these people? Soldiers? Circus performers?

Taipan hefted Anya over his shoulder as though she weighed nothing. He was small, but he was strong.

'Come with me, young man,' he said. 'And no funny business, or you and your friend will both regret it. Briefly.'

Jarli swallowed. 'She needs a doctor.'

The squat man beamed, showing a gap between his front teeth. 'How fortunate. We're on our way to see two doctors right now.'

Jarli shot a worried glance at Olivia, and followed Taipan as he carried Anya up the stairs. Taipan moved eagerly, taking the steps three at a time.

'Do you like action films?' he asked, as he walked.

It took Jarli a moment to realise the criminal was talking to him. 'What?'

'Action films. Do you like them?'

'Sometimes,' Jarli said cautiously.

'I hate them,' Taipan said. 'So unrealistic. For example, James Bond sometimes attaches a "silencer" to his gun so no-one hears the shot. In real life, that device is called a "suppressor", because the shot most definitely is not silent.'

'OK.' Jarli rubbed his sore wrist. He wasn't tied to

a bench anymore, but he couldn't shake the feeling that things were about to get worse.

At the top of the stairs, the corridor was as quiet as death. Jarli was afraid to ask where all the other doctors and patients had gone. How long before the police realised what was happening here?

'If you want to shoot someone quietly, without alerting the authorities,' Taipan continued, 'you go medieval.'

A tattooed woman was standing outside one of the operating theatres holding a rusty crossbow. It looked like it might have been stolen from a museum. Jarli found himself shuddering uncontrollably, like a car on the verge of stalling.

'What kept you?' the woman asked.

'Patience is a virtue, Mamba.' Taipan dumped Anya on the floor and Jarli flinched. Then Taipan knocked on the operating room door.

There was no answer from the other side.

'You're in luck,' Taipan shouted at the door. 'Instead of getting through this door with high explosives, we've opted to have our friend open it for us. His name is . . .'

He gestured at Jarli.

Jarli muttered, 'Jarli.'

'Louder, please.'

'Jarli.'

He heard a gasp from the other side of the door.

'Jarli will be assisted in this endeavour by . . .' Taipan pointed at Anya, slumped on the floor.

'Anya,' Jarli said.

'Here are the terms. You have sixty seconds to open the door, or Jarli dies. If the door is not open sixty seconds after that, Anya dies. Then we blast our way in with explosives. I trust you'll make the right choice.'

Mamba pointed the rusty crossbow at Jarli's head.

TWO AGAINST ONE

The squat man's voice was muffled by the door. 'Your time starts now.'

For a second, no-one moved. Bess was frozen with terror. Her phone hadn't beeped once. Taipan and Mamba weren't bluffing.

A line from a crime novel flitted through her head: *motive, means and opportunity*. The criminals had a reason, a weapon and no-one to stop them from killing Jarli and Anya.

Bess looked around. Everyone was just cowering on the floor, waiting for someone else to do something. To make this impossible decision.

Bess pushed herself to her feet.

'Bess,' Mr Hayes said. 'Get back here.'

Bess ignored him. She limped towards the door. It was hard on only one crutch. The other was still wedged tightly through the door handles—she hoped she would have the strength to get it out.

'What are you doing?' Hayes demanded.

'What are *you* doing?' she shot back. No-one else

had spoken. Were the others really willing to let Jarli and Anya die?

Lanagan looked up from her surgery. 'Don't go near that door. We can't let them hurt Mr Plowman.'

'Can we let them murder Jarli and Anya?' Bess demanded. 'Because that's what will happen if we don't open the door.'

'They might kill them even if we do,' Lanagan said. 'And the rest of us will be defenceless.'

Vorham looked from Lanagan to Bess, clearly uncertain who to side with.

Bess reached for the crutch holding the door closed. Hayes ran over and grabbed her arm. His teacherly calm was gone. His hair was scraggly, and his voice was hoarse.

'You can't,' he said.

Bess had never liked Mr Hayes. PE was her least-favourite class, because she always ended up doing nothing while everyone else had fun. She had hated every sport her parents had ever made her try—table tennis, bowling, golf, archery, fencing. Bess couldn't imagine becoming a PE teacher unless she'd already failed at every other job.

'Let go of me!' she snapped.

'I'm responsible for all these students,' Hayes said. 'If we let them in, they might kill all of us. Including Anya and Jarli.'

Bess knew he was right. But there was also a possibility that the criminals *wouldn't* do that. Jarli was her oldest friend. She couldn't do nothing. Not if there was even a slim chance of saving him.

'Time's nearly up,' Taipan said gleefully.

Bess tried to grab the crutch again, but Hayes held her still. Tears of frustration sprang into her eyes.

'Don't hurt him!' she shouted through the door. 'We're opening the door!'

'Do not,' Lanagan said. 'There's a reason that governments don't negotiate with terrorists. I'm not giving up my patient.'

Vorham said nothing, looking from Bess to Lanagan to Hayes and back again.

Doug ran over. Bess thought he was going to restrain her other arm, but no—he grabbed the crutch and tried to wrestle it out of the door. He was on her side.

'Stop!' Hayes cried.

There was a *ka-chunk* sound from outside the door.

It took Bess a second to recognise the noise. She'd heard it in a TV show.

It was the sound of a crossbow firing.

She screamed.

Fifteen seconds earlier

'Time's nearly up,' Taipan said to the door. He was leering, like a creepy clown. This was fun for him, Jarli realised.

Not Mamba. Her face may as well have been carved from stone. The crossbow was dead-still in her grip. Jarli saw now that although the device itself looked old, there was a shiny new scope attached to the top. Not that Mamba would need the scope at this range. The needle-sharp tip of the bolt hovered only centimetres from Jarli's eyeball. If she pulled the trigger, he wouldn't even hear the shot.

'You don't need to do this,' he stammered. It was hard to get the words out.

Mamba didn't move.

'They can't see us,' Jarli whispered. 'I can pretend, OK? I'll pretend you're pointing it at me.'

Mamba still didn't move.

'Should we shoot the girl first?' Taipan mused. 'So the boy screams?'

'No,' Mamba growled. 'Always deal with mobile targets first.'

'Don't hurt him!' Bess was yelling from inside the theatre. 'We're opening the door!'

Jarli hoped that was true. The bad guys weren't bluffing. Jarli's app hadn't beeped once the whole time Taipan was talking. He definitely intended to KILL them both.

Taipan glanced at his watch. Then he stepped back and nodded to Mamba.

Mamba shifted her weight, straightened her arm, and squeezed the trigger—

But just as she was about to fire, the crossbow was kicked out of her hand.

It discharged in mid-air, the mechanism snapping like a mouse trap. The bolt punched a hole in the ceiling, releasing a puff of dust.

Mamba spun, trying to see who had attacked her—

And found herself facing Anya.

Jarli stared. Anya didn't look like a girl who had been unconscious a few seconds ago. She stood like a boxer, bouncing on her toes, hands up, ready to parry away any oncoming blows.

She had been faking it, Jarli realised. So she could surprise the bad guys at the right moment. And Olivia, the paramedic, had figured that out, which was why she'd told Jarli to shut up.

Mamba swung a fist at Anya, who ducked under the blow. Another punch. Another dodge. Jarli had seen Anya do incredible things. She had climbed tall buildings to spy on corrupt politicians. She had been a finalist in the state under-eighteens boxing championship. But she couldn't fight off two trained killers by herself.

The crossbow had landed a couple of metres away. Taipan dived for it, but Jarli kicked it out of reach, hurting his toes in the process. The crossbow skittered away up the corridor.

Anya tried to sweep Mamba's legs out from under her, but Mamba was too fast and too smart. Instead of jumping back, she stepped in closer and shoved Anya's chest, sending her sprawling.

Anya landed right next to the bomb—a rectangle of soft plastic, like a lump of clay, with a timer wired to it. The numbers 00:60 were still flashing.

Taipan saw what was about to happen. 'No!'

Anya scooped up the bomb and pushed the red button on the timer. The numbers started counting down from sixty.

'Run, Jarli!' she yelled. Then she sprinted away up the corridor, carrying the bomb.

THAT AMOUNT OF CRAZY

Anya had hoped for a better moment than this.

She had thought if she pretended to be unconscious, the criminals would eventually leave her unguarded. Then she could hack through her plastic cuffs with the nail file in her pocket and go looking for something more effective to cut Jarli free. This was a hospital, so there would be big scissors for cutting stitches and staples.

But then the criminals had carried her and Jarli upstairs into an even more volatile situation, with a bomb and a crossbow. Kicking away the crossbow and stealing the bomb was all she had been able to think of.

Starting the timer on the bomb was supposed to distract the criminals so Jarli could get away. She could turn the timer off again once she was out of sight. The criminals wouldn't chase her, surely. They'd have to be crazy to run towards a live bomb.

Unfortunately, they seemed to be exactly that amount of crazy. Anya could hear Mamba's feet slapping the waxed tile floor; the woman was getting closer. *She thinks she can catch me fast enough to stop the timer before the bomb goes off,* Anya thought. *She might be right.* The man was slower, with his short legs, but he was coming too.

And there was a third pair of footsteps. When Anya risked a glance back, Jarli was running right behind her.

'What are you doing?' she cried.

'You told me to run!' Jarli puffed.

'I meant the other way!'

Ka-chunk! Another crossbow bolt flew past her head and buried itself in the wall up the other end of the corridor. Anya didn't stop running.

She and Jarli reached the end of the corridor and turned. A door up ahead was marked FIRE STAIRS. Anya barged through it sideways, cradling the bomb under one arm. The timer had ticked down to thirty seconds.

She found herself in a gloomy concrete stairwell, lit by a distant skylight. Coiled-up fire hoses were wall-mounted on every second landing. Anya ran upstairs rather than down. She was lighter than the criminals. It would be hard for them to keep up.

Unfortunately, it sounded like Jarli was struggling to keep up too. She could hear his ragged breaths echoing off the walls as they pounded up the stairs.

He was good at coding, but wasn't very athletic. Soon he would fall behind.

Anya peered over the rail in time to see Mamba burst through the stairwell door below. Mamba took aim with her crossbow again, but then Taipan charged through the door and grabbed her arm.

'Let them go!' he hissed. 'Take cover!'

As they both disappeared back through the door, Anya looked down at the timer.

00:28. 00:27. 00:26. No wonder the criminals were fleeing. Time to stop the countdown.

She hit the red button.

The countdown kept going. 00:24. 00:23. 00:22.

She tried again. No result. 00:20. 00:19.

Jarli was practically vibrating with panic. 'What are you doing?'

'I assumed I would be able to switch it off!' she cried.

'You assumed?!'

00:16. 00:15.

'Just pull out the wires!' Jarli yelled.

Anya wrapped her hand around the cords, but hesitated. What if that set the bomb off?

00:13. 00:12.

'What are you waiting for?' Jarli demanded.

'I have a better idea!' Anya sprinted up the next

flight of stairs towards the roof.

She shoved open the door at the top of the stairs and found herself on the roof—a flat concrete plain dotted only by air-conditioning units and antennae. The storm had reached full force. Wind whipped at Anya's hair as raindrops exploded on the concrete all around her. Thunder boomed like orchestral drums.

Anya sprinted over to the edge and wobbled. It was a long way down. At least ten metres. A vortex of raindrops plummeted past her to the puddles on the distant concrete.

00:07. 00:06. 00:05.

Anya frantically looked around for the best place to throw the bomb. Not straight down—Lanagan had mentioned flammable cladding inside the walls. The whole hospital could catch fire. Not towards the car park, either. Someone could be in one of those cars. Not towards the bush on the other side—not unless she wanted to be showered with sharp chunks of trees and dead animals. But there was a broad grassy plain between the forest and the car park. EMPTY.

00:03. 00:02.

Anya hurled the bomb as far as she could. Then she lay facedown on the concrete with her hands over her ears. Jarli did the same.

For a moment, the only sound was the rain.

And then—

BLAM! The bomb exploded in mid-air with a sound like a whip crack which echoed from the distant hills. The shockwave ruffled Anya's clothes and sent hot raindrops sideways. A mist of smoke stung her nose.

When Anya looked up, there was no sign that the bomb had ever existed. She peered over the edge. The grass had been scorched, but nothing else looked damaged. The bomb had been designed to blast open a door. She guessed that the criminals wouldn't have wanted too much power.

'That was *way* too close,' Jarli was saying.

Anya released the breath she had been holding. 'I agree.'

'Someone in town must have heard that. The cops will be coming. Right?'

Anya looked towards the centre of town, shielding her eyes from the rain with one hand. She couldn't see any flashing lights or hear any sirens. Just her luck to end up in a town so sleepy that a bomb could go off and no-one would notice.

'It probably sounded like thunder,' she said. 'To everyone except the bad guys. They will be up here to get us soon. Do you have a phone signal?'

Jarli pulled out his phone and checked the screen. 'No. They're blocking our phones with a jammer.'

'What sort of range would that have?'

'I dunno. About the same as a wi-fi router, probably. Twenty to forty metres, but there could be more than one. Hang on.' Jarli ran over to the nearest radio antenna, which stuck out of the roof like a leafless tree.

'What are you doing?' Anya asked.

Jarli was tracing the cables down to the power source. 'This antenna would have a signal booster built into it,' he said. 'If I can disconnect it from the hospital line and plug in my phone instead, that might get my signal beyond the range of the jammer. Got a screwdriver?'

Anya shook her head.

Jarli peered down at the metal plate which fixed the antenna to the roof. 'The booster would be under there. Maybe we could just . . . bash through it somehow.'

Anya ran back into the stairwell and grabbed the fire hose. It was coiled up on a giant wheel, designed to unspool quickly and easily. The nozzle was heavy steel. It might work.

She left the stairwell door slightly ajar and ran back out to Jarli, unspooling the fire hose as she went.

Jarli banged the nozzle against the metal plate. It left a scratch but didn't break through.

'Let me try.' Anya swung the nozzle. *Clang*. Another scratch.

Footsteps echoed from the stairwell. The door burst all the way open. Mamba stepped out with her crossbow raised, her face contorted with anger. Taipan was right behind her, looking puffed.

'Kill them!' he gasped.

Mamba aimed the crossbow.

Anya quickly wrapped the fire hose around her arm. 'Jump!' she cried. And without waiting to see if Jarli had understood, she hugged him and leapt off the roof.

GETAWAY DRIVER

Jarli couldn't even scream. Anya was squeezing him too tight, and he was squeezing her right back. They plummeted upside-down towards the ground, the fire hose ribboning through the air. The wall sped past like a speeding train, windows flitting upwards.

An ambulance was parked below. The roof looked hard, but Jarli thought they would miss it. Unfortunately, the concrete next to it looked harder.

Snap! The hose jerked taut just before they hit the ground. Jarli felt Anya's arms tighten around him as they bounced in the air and swung sideways into the ambulance. Jarli's head hit the door hard enough to leave a dent. He lost his grip on Anya. They both tumbled to the ground and lay still. The world spun. For a minute Jarli felt like he was still falling.

Anya was already scrambling towards the ambulance. Jarli crawled woozily after her. They crouched behind it, out of sight of the roof.

Just in time. A crossbow bolt pinged off the top of the ambulance. Mamba was firing from the rooftop.

'We're trapped,' Jarli hissed. 'What do we do?'

Anya pulled out her phone. She stabbed at the screen and groaned with frustration. 'Does yours work?'

Jarli checked his phone. No signal. 'We need to get further away from the jammer.'

Another bolt struck the ambulance. 'We're stuck here,' Anya said. 'If we run—'

Jarli heard the *whoosh* of sliding doors. Someone was coming out of the hospital. Probably Rattler, the woman with the sword who had been guarding the front entrance.

He looked around for a way to escape. If they stayed here, they would be caught. But if they left the cover of the ambulance, they could be shot from the roof.

Which left only one possibility.

Anya was closest to the driver's side door of the ambulance.

'Are the keys in that thing?' Jarli whispered.

Anya's eyes widened. She raised her head and peeped through the window. Then she nodded at Jarli.

'OK, get in!' Jarli hissed.

Anya opened the door and slipped in, crawling across to the passenger seat. Jarli followed. He heard Rattler's footsteps getting faster—she had realised what they were doing.

Jarli slammed the door closed. Rattler appeared at the glass a split-second later. She reached for the handle, but Jarli locked the door just in time. *Click*. Rattler pulled on the handle, bracing her foot against the side of the ambulance. The door creaked. Then the handle snapped off in Rattler's grip, and she tumbled over backwards.

'Do you know how to drive?' Anya asked urgently.

Jarli was in the driver's seat. He looked at the controls. He knew how the steering wheel and the pedals worked, but the rest looked alien. In a country town like Kelton, a lot of kids had practised driving, but Jarli wasn't one of them. A golf cart was the closest he'd come to driving a real car.

'How hard could it be?' he asked, and twisted the key.

The engine started purring. Lights blinked on across the dashboard.

Rattler raised her sword and charged at Jarli's window. She was going to smash the glass.

'Go!' Anya yelled.

Jarli slammed his foot on what he thought was the accelerator. The ambulance lurched, but didn't actually go anywhere. Something beeped and a warning light flashed. HANDBRAKE. Jarli looked around frantically. *Where's the handbrake?*

Rattler struck the handle of her sword against the window. Glass shattered into slivers and her other hand snaked in, grabbing Jarli's shirt. He screamed as she tried to pull him out the window.

Anya found the handbrake and released it. The ambulance jerked forwards, dragging Rattler off her feet. She clung to Jarli through the window as the ambulance bumped over the curb and onto the scorched grass.

Jarli spun the wheel. The ambulance swerved left. Rattler's grip loosened, and then she was gone, sucked out the window by the centrifugal force.

'Turn! Turn!' Anya cried.

Jarli looked up at the windscreen in time to see that the ambulance was hurtling towards a solid-looking tree. He stamped on the brake pedal and spun the wheel at the same time. The ambulance went into a skid, churning up the mud until the wheels caught. It stopped just in time to avoid the tree trunk.

THWACK! A crossbow bolt punctured the side of the ambulance and got stuck halfway through the metal. Jarli shielded the side of his face with one arm and planted his foot on the accelerator again. The ambulance started bouncing down the hill towards the road.

He had to shout to be heard over the wind roaring

through the broken window. 'Does your phone have a signal yet?'

Anya held her phone up in the air. 'No.'

'What about that radio?' Jarli pointed to a complicated-looking device on the dashboard.

Anya prodded some buttons. 'I don't know how it works.'

Jarli steered the ambulance onto the road. The rain had eased off to a light mist, but the asphalt was still wet and slippery. He slowed right down. There was no other traffic.

'We must be out of range by now,' he said. 'Try the phone again.'

Anya peered at the screed. 'Still no signal.'

'How can that be?' Jarli demanded. 'The range of the jammer should be less than—'

He broke off as he realised what this meant. Fear stabbed his heart. A jammer was *following* them.

He looked in the side-mirror and saw a four-wheel drive hurtling down the hill with Rattler behind the wheel. She was catching up to them, fast. A message on the mirror caught Jarli's eye: **OBJECTS IN MIRROR ARE CLOSER THAN THEY APPEAR.**

'Hold on to something!' he yelled.

SMASH! The 4WD rammed the back of the ambulance, shunting it forwards. Jarli's head hit the headrest and his hands flew off the steering wheel. The sudden ringing in his ears drowned out whatever Anya was trying to say. He tried to look at her, but realised he couldn't move his neck.

His legs worked fine, though. So he pushed his foot down on the accelerator.

Broken glass jingled outside, maybe from the tail lights of the ambulance. Then they were zooming forwards again, along the road towards the town.

Have to get out of range, Jarli thought. *Gotta call for help.*

The 4WD shrank in the rear-view mirror—

Then it started to grow again. Giving chase.

Jarli found himself hurtling towards Kelton at top speed in a stolen ambulance, trying to outrun the criminal who had just rammed him. Where had today gone wrong?

'Anya,' he shouted. 'You OK?'

'I still have no phone signal.' Anya's voice was barely audible over the roar of two engines going flat out.

'Send a text message to Constable Blanco.' Jarli pulled out his phone, unlocked it with his thumb-print and held it out until he felt Anya take it. Blanco was the only cop in his contacts list.

'No signal. A text message will not go through.'

'Try anyway.'

Behind them, the 4WD was getting closer. It was

trying to ram the ambulance again. Jarli abruptly swerved left onto a suburban street. A sedan was parked on the street a few houses up. Jarli tried to avoid it, and almost succeeded. The ambulance knocked off a side-mirror as it screamed past, showering the street with BROKEN GLASS.

'Whoops,' Jarli said.

Anya was typing. *'Kelton hospital taken over by four armed criminals. School kids held hostage. Hurry.'* Anything else I should add?'

'No. Send it.'

Anya tried. 'Sending failed,' she said.

'Chuck the phone out the window,' Jarli said.

'What?!'

'Onto one of those lawns. Quick!'

Now Anya seemed to understand. She wound down her window and tossed the phone. Jarli didn't see where it landed—hopefully somewhere soft. The phone would keep trying to send the message. As soon as the jammer was out of range, it would go through.

The 4WD had caught up again. Jarli clung to the steering wheel, gritting his teeth. The bull bar of the 4WD nudged the back of the ambulance, knocking it off course.

'Hang on!' Jarli cried.

The ambulance ploughed through a pair of

wheelie bins, showering the windscreen with pizza boxes, shattered plastic and a splurt of rancid milk. The smell was disgusting. Jarli steered blindly, unable to see through the garbage. He couldn't find the switch for the windscreen wipers.

Anya poked her head out the window. 'Tree!' she shouted.

Jarli slammed on the brakes. The ambulance skidded over a driveway and hit something—the tree, maybe—with a hard *thud*. The airbag exploded out of the steering wheel like a mushroom cloud and thumped Jarli in the face. He rocked back in his seat, gasping.

Anya was already fighting her way out of the seatbelt. 'Run!' she cried.

Jarli pushed the airbag away and grabbed the doorhandle. His eyes were streaming from the force of the airbag hitting his nose. Finally the door popped open and he fell out onto the road.

'Split up,' he yelled. 'She can't chase both of us.'

He turned to run, but his legs collapsed under him. The crash had turned his muscles to jelly. He hit the ground like a puppet with cut strings.

'Look,' Anya said, pointing.

Jarli rolled over and looked.

The 4WD was gone.

SEARCH AND RESCUE

Ten minutes earlier

Bess heard the blast even through the thick walls of the hospital. Something, somewhere, had gotten blown up.

Possibly her oldest friend.

Her whole body shook. It wasn't like her normal tremors and spasms. It was as though every nerve in her body had frayed and was shooting sparks. None of her limbs were listening to her brain. She didn't even realise she was on the floor until Doug was standing over her.

'Bess. You OK?'

She tried to tell him she was fine—she didn't want his help—but her jaw had locked up.

Doug crouched down next to her and took her hand. 'You're having a panic attack,' he whispered. 'It feels life-threatening, but it's not. You're going to be OK. Just wait it out.'

Bess couldn't breathe. Her palms had gone clammy. What if Jarli was dead?

Something roared somewhere outside. An engine. The other students squeaked with terror, cowering in the corners of the room.

'Think of a song you know.' Doug kept his voice low. So far, no-one else had noticed Bess's distress. 'Try to remember the words. That always helps me.'

Bess tried to think of something. But it felt like she was having a heart attack. How was she supposed to come up with a song while her whole body was seizing up?

'How about "Girls Like You"?' Doug suggested. He hummed a few bars of it, very badly. Bess would have laughed if she wasn't so scared.

'Jarli,' Bess managed to say. *And Anya,* she thought suddenly. The guilt winded her. It shouldn't have taken her so long to worry about Anya.

'I know,' Doug was saying. 'I'm worried, too. But we'll figure something out together. OK?'

'OK.' Bess closed her eyes. She listened to her own breaths, cool on the way in, warm on the way out. Her galloping heart slowed to a canter.

That was the worst, she thought. She'd never had a panic attack before. It was weird to think of Doug having them. He hardly ever looked scared.

'You alright?' Doug asked.

Bess nodded and sat up, rubbing her sweaty hands on her pants. 'Thanks.'

'When my family first came to Kelton,' Doug said, 'I used to have moments like that. I'd see the same car twice, or I'd notice someone walking in the same direction as me, or I'd hear noises outside my bedroom window—and I'd think Viper had found us.'

Bess knew that Doug had been in witness protection, but she hadn't thought about how scary it must have been. 'How did you get past that?' she asked.

'Well, Viper *did* find us,' Doug said. 'Hard to be scared when the worst has already happened. Now he knows where we are, and I just . . . live with it, I guess.'

When Bess looked around, she saw that the doctors had barely reacted to the noise of the explosion. They were both bent over Mr Plowman like mechanics examining an engine. Plowman was covered in so many sheets that Bess could hardly see him. The bright lights made the bed hard to look at.

'More internal bleeding here, under the eighth rib,' Lanagan was saying. 'And tissue damage on this lung. Is that a pacemaker? I've never seen one like it.'

'Focus on the stitches,' Vorham said. 'This is the last transfusion.'

'What do you mean?'

'After this bag, we're out of O-negative blood.'

Lanagan didn't respond to that, but Bess could sense her anxiety. It sounded like Plowman wasn't going to make it.

Horrified, Bess looked at the half-empty bag of donor blood, slowly trickling down a tube into Plowman's arm. They had sent Nurse Amon to get more, but he hadn't come back—the criminals must have caught him. Plowman was dying in front of them, and there was nothing they could do.

'Hey,' Doug said suddenly. 'Are the bad guys still outside the door?'

The whole room fell silent. Bess realised she hadn't heard the criminals say anything since Anya had shouted, 'Run, Jarli!' There had been a flurry of footsteps fading into the distance, and then nothing.

Maybe the door was unguarded.

'Is there more donor blood?' Doug was asking. 'Somewhere else in the hospital?'

Lanagan nodded. 'You remember the hazardous materials room? Next door to that is an equipment storage area. We keep blood in a fridge in there.'

'But we can't get it,' Vorham said. 'Donor blood is no good to a corpse. This patient needs full attention from both myself and Dr Lanagan.'

'I'll go,' Doug said.

Everyone looked at him.

'The fridge in the storage area right next to the hazardous materials room,' he said. 'O-negative, right?'

'Right,' Lanagan said.

'No. You're in my care right now,' said Mr Hayes, the PE teacher. 'Sorry, Doug—but, legally, I can't let you leave.'

'Is it legal to just let that guy die?' Doug asked.

'If the alternative means risking your life, yes.'

'That's a dumb law,' Doug said, crossing the room to the door.

'Wait.' Mr Hayes got up off the floor and started moving towards Doug. But Doug was already pulling out the crutch to unlock the door.

'Be careful,' Bess told him.

'I will.' Doug opened the door and slipped out.

CHANGE OF PLAN

Doug looked up and down the corridor. No sign of the criminals. But they would be around somewhere. He had to be quick.

He slipped off his shoes and sprinted silently up the corridor, carrying them in one hand, socks stuffed inside. The tiles felt cool under his bare feet.

He reached a corner and peeked around it. No-one. But he could hear voices. It sounded like Taipan and Mamba were coming back.

Doug hesitated. If he ran back the way he came, he might make it to the surgical theatre before the criminals arrived. But then he'd be trapped there again. And without another blood transfusion, Plowman would die.

There was a cleaning closet just around the corner. Doug tried the handle. Unlocked. He pulled the door open, slipped inside and closed the door gently behind him.

It was pitch black in the closet. The smell of bleach was overpowering. Doug didn't risk trying to find a light switch. Instead, he covered his mouth and nose with one arm while he held the door closed with his other hand. If they tried the door, hopefully the criminals would think the closet was locked.

Their footsteps came closer. Soon Doug could hear what they were saying:

'. . . think Viper wants with this stuff?'

'Not our problem. But don't drop the canister. I don't feel like dying today. What's that?'

'A message from Rattler. She says the police have been alerted. They'll be here in ten.'

'I thought Viper was keeping them distracted on the other side of Kelton?'

'Right, but this stupid town is barely twenty kilometres across. And there's something else. Apparently a signal is getting through the jammers somehow.'

'A message?'

'No. A sound like a HEARTBEAT. Probably just interference from some medical equipment.'

'Well, send a message to Viper about it, just in case. And tell Rattler to come back. No point chasing those two kids. The cat's out of the bag.'

'Viper's going to be mad.'

'He knows these jobs never go exactly to plan. As long as Plowman is dead and the flask gets delivered, Viper will be happy. Where's Anaconda?'

Their voices faded away. It sounded like they were going back to the theatre. That was bad news. If they were standing guard outside it, Doug wouldn't be able to get back in and deliver the blood. He would have to distract them somehow.

But all that would come later. He could practically hear his mother's voice, as they sat on opposite sides of the plastic travel chessboard: 'Focus on each move. Long term plans rely too much on the other player. You win chess one move at a time.'

Find the blood, Doug told himself. *Without it, there's no point going back.*

He slowly opened the closet door. The corridor was empty now. He slipped out and kept running towards the hazardous materials chamber.

The storage room was next to it, as the doctors had said. He slipped through the door, and found himself in a cramped room full of supplies—sheets, bandages, packaged syringes, bottles of disinfectant.

The stainless steel fridge up the back turned out to be full of blood. Dozens of bags of it, so much that Doug felt a bit faint.

He swallowed his nausea and rummaged through the bags, scooping up all the ones marked TYPE O NEGATIVE. The label also said 'universal donor'. Maybe the doctors still didn't know Plowman's blood type.

He could only carry six bags. He hoped it would be enough. With his pockets and his hands full, he slipped out of the storage room. So far, so good.

Doug slowed down as he ran back towards the theatre, listening for voices. But he couldn't hear anything. If the criminals were guarding the theatre, they weren't talking.

Doug risked a peek around the corner. There was no-one. Just the fading outlines of his sweaty footprints from earlier. The criminals must have gone somewhere else.

Unable to believe his luck, Doug sprinted up to the theatre doors and knocked urgently. 'It's me!' he hissed. 'Quick! Let me in!'

He heard someone fiddling with the crutch to unlock the doors. It opened to reveal Bess—

But Doug had been tricked.

A crossbow bolt shot out of the shadows at the far end of the stairwell. It rebounded off a metal ceiling beam and thunked into the floor between the open doors, narrowly missing Doug's foot. With a sharp *splink* sound, prongs flipped out of the sides, as if the bolt had sprouted thorns.

'Get inside!' Bess yelled.

Doug scrambled into the theatre. He dumped the blood bags on the table next to Plowman while Bess and Hayes attempted to close the doors. But the crossbow bolt was in the way. It had been aimed perfectly.

Doug ran back and tried to rip the bolt out of the floor, but the thorns made it impossible to grip. And then suddenly it was too late.

Two hands shot through the gap and grabbed him.

Bess screamed as the two criminals stormed into the surgical theatre. Taipan was holding up a grenade. Mamba pointed her crossbow at the two doctors.

'Back away from the patient,' she said.

The two doctors reluctantly raised their gloved hands.

'We're just barely keeping him alive right now,' Lanagan said.

Mamba fired a bolt into the ceiling. The room filled with screams as the doctor scuttled back.

Taipan threw Doug aside. 'You know, if you'd let us in earlier,' he said, 'you could have saved everyone a good deal of trouble.'

Doug climbed to his feet. He looked shaken, but not hurt. He ran over to Bess and leaned in close to her.

'You OK?' Bess whispered.

'Yeah—and so are Jarli and Anya. I heard the bad guys talking. They got away.'

A rush of relief swept through Bess's body. Jarli was free!

Taipan's phone rang. He pulled it out of his pocket. It was a strange looking thing, bristling with antennae. Bess guessed that this was one of the jammers—but she hadn't realised that it would be able to make and receive calls.

If she could steal it, they could call the police.

Bess started edging towards Taipan. It was hard to move stealthily on her crutches—but she knew from experience that they also made her semi-invisible. She was often ignored or underestimated. And people with phones in their hands never paid much attention to their surroundings.

'It's Viper,' Taipan said, looking down at the screen. He sounded almost frightened. 'Probably wondering what's taking so long.'

'Tell him we're nearly done,' Mamba growled. She stormed over to Plowman, crossbow raised.

'Don't!' Lanagan cried, throwing herself in front of her patient.

Taipan swallowed, and answered the phone. 'I'm here.'

Bess heard a distorted voice, tinny in the phone speakers. She couldn't make out the words.

Mamba pushed Lanagan aside, and she sprawled on the floor. Mamba pointed the crossbow at Plowman's head—

'Wait!' Taipan yelled.

Mamba froze. 'What?'

'Understood,' Taipan said into the phone. Then he ended the call and pointed at the two doctors.

'Change of plan,' he said. 'You two are going to save Kellin Plowman's life. If he dies, so do you.'

PART TWO: CRISIS

'THE APP STRUGGLES WITH COMPULSIVE LIARS, BECAUSE THEY DON'T CARE ABOUT GETTING CAUGHT OUT. THEY'RE NOT NERVOUS, THEY DON'T USE EVASIVE LANGUAGE, THEY'RE NOT EVEN NECESSARILY CONCENTRATING. FORTUNATELY, PEOPLE LIKE THAT TEND TO GET EXPOSED FAIRLY QUICKLY. YOU DON'T NEED AN APP TO IDENTIFY THEM.'

—*From the documentation for* Truth, *version 4.2*

MISSING A DAY

'Didn't seem so far,' Anya puffed, 'in the ambulance.'

Jarli could only nod. They were heading back through Kelton towards the hospital. The distance had only taken them a few minutes to drive, but it had been mostly downhill. Now they were on foot, shuffling uphill like exhausted marathon runners, and it seemed to be taking forever. At least the rain kept them cool.

Jarli could hardly breathe and he had a thumping headache. He wasn't sure if it was exertion or stress. A lot could have happened in the hospital since he and Anya fled. Mr Plowman might have died. His friends could be—

Don't think about it, he told himself.

They had searched for his phone, but weren't sure whose front garden it had landed in, and everyone on that street seemed to have dense hedges. Anya had tried to call it on her phone, but they heard nothing. When she dialled the local police, no-one picked up. A recorded message told her to leave her contact details.

Since they'd been walking, they'd seen a number of police cars speed past. But Jarli and Anya still had no idea what they would find when they got back to the hospital. A building surrounded by cops? A bunch of rescued hostages? A crater where the building used to be?

This morning, Jarli had gotten up expecting a normal day at school. Now he'd been stunned by a flash grenade, shot at with a crossbow, knocked off a roof, chased in a stolen ambulance—and it wasn't even 4 p.m. yet. No wonder his head was pounding.

'I never could get the hang of Thursdays,' Jarli muttered.

'It's Friday,' Anya said.

'I was quoting *The Hitchhiker's Guide to the Galaxy,*' Jarli said. Although he was pretty sure Anya was wrong. Yesterday had definitely been Wednesday . . .

Or had it? Olivia's voice echoed through his head: *A van dropped you off in front of the video store. You looked lost. I asked if you were OK.* Had he lost a day somehow? Maybe he was in shock.

'Keep an eye out for Rattler's car,' Anya said as they ran. 'Could still be around.'

'Maybe.' But the vehicle had disappeared pretty soon after he sent the text message. Rattler had probably given up when she heard the sirens.

Suddenly Jarli realised he'd only seen three of the four bad guys. Rattler, Mamba and Taipan. The fourth one, Anaconda, was a mystery. If the police needed to know about the criminals and their weapons, he would only be able to describe three of them.

As they rounded a corner, the hospital came into view on top of the hill, the white walls standing out against the dark clouds. Police drones hovered around the building, monitoring the exits from the air. Cop cars were all around, red and blue lights flashing.

Jarli was relieved to see so many police officers here, talking into radios and surveying the hospital through binoculars. The criminals were outnumbered. This wasn't his problem anymore.

But that didn't mean the hostages were safe.

'Wow,' Anya said.

'Yeah.' Jarli bent over, hugging his knees as he caught his breath. 'I guess we need to find someone to talk to, tell them what we know.'

A few non-police cars were parked nearby, probably belonging to the hospital staff. But one of them, a green Fiat, was occupied.

'Jarli,' Anya said. 'Isn't that your friend? The reporter?'

Jarli looked. Yes—Dana Reynolds was behind the wheel, peering at the hospital through binoculars. No other reporters or media were visible—when Viper was involved, Reynolds always somehow managed to be first on the scene.

'She's not really my friend,' Jarli said. She had helped him once or twice, but only when it gave her a scoop. If she saw him and Anya, she would insist on interviewing them both. 'We need to talk to the cops.'

'Do you see the police officer we sent the text message to? Constable Blanco?'

'Uh, she's suspended,' Jarli said. 'So she's probably not here.'

Anya blinked. 'Wait—we sent that message to a suspended officer?'

'Yeah.'

'Suspended for what?'

Jarli shuffled his feet awkwardly. 'Suspected connections to Viper.'

Anya grabbed his collar. He had never seen her look so angry. 'So, after four criminals with snake-themed codenames took over the hospital,' she began, 'you decided it would be a good idea to—'

'Hey! Firstly, we were kind of in a hurry and she was the only cop saved in my contacts. Secondly, it's obvious that she did the right thing with the information—every cop in Kelton is here. Thirdly, without her help, we wouldn't have escaped from Viper the first time he showed up in Kelton. So she can be trusted.'

Anya released him. 'OK. I am sorry.'

Jarli exhaled. 'It's cool.'

'But if she is not here, who do we talk to?'

'Dunno.'

They walked up the hill towards the commotion.

A burly police officer with a goatee saw them and approached. 'Sorry kids,' he said. 'This building is locked down. If you need medical attention you'll have to go to the regional hospital.'

'No,' Jarli said. 'We're the ones who called you guys.'

'We were inside when the criminals arrived,' Anya added. 'We have information about them.'

The officer checked his phone. Plowman hadn't wanted to tell the police that they knew *Truth Premium* was compromised, but Jarli had warned them anyway. He was annoyed to see that some officers still used it.

'Alrighty, then.' The officer pocketed his phone. 'Follow me.'

He led them further up the hill where a woman was talking on the phone and peering at a map she had spread across the boot of her car. The raindrops appeared to be shredding it. Jarli recognised the woman and his heart sank. It was Detective Zee Arno. They had met several times. She had once arrested him for attempted murder.

'I don't understand,' she said into the phone. 'What kind of device is it coming from?'

There was a pause.

'Firstly, how is the signal beating the jammers? Secondly, how would anyone use a pacemaker to transmit data? Thirdly, why would they even try?'

'Maybe they're tracking their heart rate,' Jarli said. 'Like a fitness thing.'

The burly officer cleared his throat. 'Excuse me, Detective Arno. These two kids have information about the assailants.'

The detective looked Jarli and Anya up and down. 'OK,' she said into the phone. 'Prep the gas and call me back when you have some answers.' She hung up. 'Jarli Durras. I'm surprised to see you.'

It took a few minutes for Jarli and Anya to tell their story. Detective Arno listened intently without interrupting.

'So,' she said, when they finished. 'When you left there was one criminal guarding the front entrance, another guarding the back and two more keeping the hostages in place. Weapons include a sword, a crossbow, some flash grenades and other explosives. Is that all correct?'

'Yes,' Anya said. 'But we did not see Anaconda. So we do not know what weapons he or she has.'

'Understood. Thanks, kids—we'll take it from here. I'll get one of my officers to give you a ride home. Rodney!'

The burly officer lumbered back up the hill towards them.

'Wait,' Jarli said. 'What was that you were saying about a pacemaker?'

The detective hesitated. 'It's complicated. We thought the criminals were using frequency jammers to block radio signals by broadcasting static on every channel. But our cyber-crime analysts say it's not just static—it's encrypted information.'

'What kind of information?' Anya asked.

Jarli knew what the detective was going to say.

'It's impossible to tell,' she replied. 'All we know is that the criminals are communicating with someone outside the hospital.'

Viper, Jarli thought.

'There's more,' the detective said. 'A second signal is coming from inside, getting around the jammer somehow. It's a heartbeat, with some metadata we can't decipher.'

'Someone is transmitting a heartbeat?' Jarli said. 'Why?'

'We don't know for sure. But it's possible that it's

a dead man's switch.'

'A what?'

'Like an insurance policy. A device outside the hospital could be monitoring the signal. If the heartbeat stops, it triggers something.' She glanced at her watch. 'You kids better get out of here.'

'Wait,' Jarli said. 'What are you going to do?'

'Don't worry,' the detective told him. 'It's under control.'

'What does that mean? Are you going in?'

'No.' She turned back to the map. 'It's too risky now that the criminals have control of a bioweapon.'

Jarli and Anya looked at each other.

'What bioweapon?' Anya asked.

'I've been informed that the hospital is storing samples which could cause mass casualties if they went airborne.'

Jarli remembered Dr Lanagan's lecture on botulism H—the deadliest substance in the world.

'We can't enter the building,' Detective Arno continued, 'or the terrorists might decide to release one or all of those samples. Thousands—potentially millions—of lives are at stake here.'

Jarli hadn't really been thinking of the criminals as 'terrorists'. 'I think they're only after Mr Plowman,' he said. 'I didn't hear them say anything about the dangerous substances room.'

'I can't take that chance,' Arno said, without looking up. 'We'll have to gas the building, catch them by surprise. Then we'll go in.'

Jarli recoiled. 'But . . . won't gassing the building also gas all the hostages?'

'It's a non-lethal gas. Should just knock them out.'

'"Should"?'

The detective said nothing.

'Mr Plowman is both wounded and anesthetised,' Anya said. 'And many of the hostages are teenagers who are smaller than the criminals. If you use enough gas to knock out healthy adults, won't that—'

'You're just gonna have to trust us.' Arno signalled Rodney, who grabbed Jarli and Anya by the shoulders.

'Come on, kids,' he said. 'Time to go.'

He frogmarched them back down the hill towards the cordon and opened the door of a police car.

'Where do you live?' he asked. 'I'll drive you home.'

Jarli caught Anya's eye. He didn't want to go home, and it looked like she didn't, either. But the app would make it hard to convince Rodney they were leaving.

'Our friend's mother owns a taxi company,' Anya said. True. 'She's always happy to come pick us up.' Also true.

Rodney looked surprised. 'I don't mind driving you.'

'Yes, but aren't you needed here?' Jarli suggested.

Rodney nodded slowly. 'OK. Well, let me know if your friend's mum can't come.'

'Thanks.'

He trudged back up the hill towards Detective Arno.

'Nice work,' Jarli whispered. 'Now what do we do?'

'We can't let them pump that gas into the building,' Anya said. 'The Russian government tried something similar during a hostage crisis in Moscow. The gas was more deadly than the criminals.'

'But they won't listen to us. We're kids.'

On the road, a blue hatchback turned off towards the hospital driveway. But the driveway was blocked by a parked police car, so the hatchback stopped at the bottom of the hill. The driver got out, carrying a bunch of roses.

It was Maria Eaton, the school nurse. Jarli was relieved to see her. Eaton was a no-nonsense ex-army medic who had helped him and his friends get out of a few tricky spots. Maybe she could talk the police out of doing anything crazy.

Eaton looked up at the police vehicles surrounding the hospital. Her eyes widened.

Jarli ran down the hill towards her, and Anya followed. 'Miss Eaton! What are you doing here?'

'Visiting a friend.' Eaton waved the flowers.

Anya's phone beeped. LIE

Eaton cleared her throat. 'OK, not *just* a friend. What's going on?'

'Four armed criminals entered the building and took everyone hostage,' Anya said. 'We were here on the science excursion, but we managed to escape.'

Eaton's mouth fell open. '*What?* Did anyone else get out?'

'No, just us,' Jarli said.

'So you're saying everyone except you is still trapped inside? Even the patients?'

Anya nodded.

The words spilled out of Jarli non-stop, like water from a broken tap. 'We called the cops and now they're here but they want to gas the building and that might kill our friends and they won't listen to us!'

'Did you say "gas the building"?' Eaton asked. 'With what?'

'Dunno. They didn't say.'

Eaton would have experienced plenty of emergencies in the army. But even so, she was starting to look worried. 'That's not good. I don't know of any airborne anaesthetic which could reliably knock out the criminals without a risk of killing somebody. The gap between ineffective and fatal is always narrow.'

'You were an army doctor,' Jarli said. 'You can talk them out of it. Right?'

'I'll definitely try,' Eaton said. 'But I suspect they won't listen to me.'

'Then what do we do?' Anya asked.

Eaton hesitated. Then she said, 'Maybe there's another option.'

Jarli tried not to sound desperate. 'Like what?'

'The police will use the air-conditioning system to circulate the gas. That's what my unit would have done. There's no other way to get it to every room. But if the aircon got switched off, they wouldn't be able to do it.'

Jarli looked at the side of the building. He couldn't see anything which looked like an air-conditioning system. 'Where would the off-switch be?'

'In a building like this? Probably in the centre. The police won't be able to get to it.'

'The criminals are using some kind of device which blocks radio signals,' Anya said. 'We can't contact the people inside.'

'No,' Eaton said. 'But do you see that? Next to the oxygen tank?'

She pointed at two big storage tanks beside the

front entrance. Just around the corner, Jarli saw a large pipe protruding from the side of the building.

'That looks like an intake tube for the aircon system,' Eaton said. 'The pipe would eventually lead to the control room. An adult wouldn't fit through, though.'

She let that hang in the air.

'You're saying we could sneak back into the building and turn off the aircon?' Jarli said. 'And then the cops couldn't use the gas?'

'Legally I can't tell you to do that,' Eaton said carefully. 'I can't even suggest it. I'm just saying that the pipe is there. And that I'm about to try to convince the police not to use the gas. While I'm doing that, they're likely to be distracted.'

'If someone crawled in there and managed to shut down the aircon in time, what then?' Anya said. 'The criminals are still inside. Some kids might be small enough to use the pipe to escape the building, but the hospital staff and Mr Hayes would not fit. Your friend and all the other patients probably could not get out that way either.'

And Bess, Jarli thought. *She couldn't climb through that.*

Eaton spread her hands wide. 'I don't know what would happen after that. I'm just saying that if the aircon stays active and that building gets gassed, there may be no survivors. Saving a few people might be better than saving none.'

Jarli bit his lip. He wasn't sure what to do. The police had told him to go home. But he didn't trust Detective Arno to keep his friends safe. She had made it clear that she would do whatever it took to stop the criminals from getting their hands on the contents of the dangerous materials room.

Eaton met his gaze. 'I'm going to talk to the police now,' she said. 'Maybe I can convince them not to use the gas. Maybe not. Either way, I hope they'll at least give me their full attention.'

She turned to go.

'What's your friend's name?' Jarli asked.

'Who?'

'The person you came to visit. Maybe we'll find them inside.'

Eaton hesitated. Then she said, 'Don't get side-tracked, and don't get sentimental. If you're going to survive this, you'll need all your wits about you.'

BREAK-IN

'Are we really doing this?' Anya asked.

Jarli watched Eaton hike up the hill towards Arno, Rodney and the other police. He wasn't sure how long she would be able to distract them for.

He swallowed. 'I can go in by myself,' he said. 'There's no need for us both to—'

'You need backup,' Anya said. 'And those are my friends in there too, by the way.'

Relieved, Jarli took a deep breath and nodded. 'OK. You ready?'

'Wait.' Anya grabbed his arm. She was watching the sky. 'We have to time this perfectly.'

The sun was getting lower behind the hill, and the hospital had a long shadow. They would be able to approach in darkness. But a police helicopter was circling, and it had switched on a searchlight. The beam swept across the hospital and the hillside.

Jarli glanced at the police. Rodney noticed Eaton approaching first. He nudged Detective Arno. She turned to look.

Now neither of the police officers were looking in the direction of the two kids.

'Wait . . .' Anya said again, still watching the helicopter. 'Wait . . . now!'

They scurried up the hill into the hospital's shadow like mice sneaking through a cat's backyard. The grass was long, but not quite thick enough to hide in. They kept their heads down and hoped for the best. Jarli wished his footsteps weren't quite so noisy.

Then headlights zoomed across the grass towards them. A vehicle was coming.

'Down!' Jarli hissed.

They both flopped facedown onto the ground. Wet grass tickled Jarli's ear. He heard a big diesel engine rumbling, louder and louder—

And then some hydraulic brakes hissed and the engine shut off.

Jarli parted the grass for a peek. It was a big truck, like a petrol tanker. A fat hose was fixed to the side of the tank. A single word was painted on the side: **CAUTION.**

Anya had seen it too. 'Gas truck,' she whispered. 'We have to hurry.'

The headlights shut off, and darkness fell again.

'Go,' Jarli muttered. They stood up and kept running.

Now that Jarli could see the pipe a bit better, he wasn't even sure they would fit. The opening was only about half a metre across. And it was at Jarli's head height—climbing in would be hard.

As they approached the hospital, a distant whining got louder and louder. The helicopter was coming back.

Jarli ran as fast as he could. He and Anya skirted around the two giant storage canisters—one marked AIR, the other O_2—and hit the wall just as the drone swept past above. They were right under the protruding pipe—it wasn't big enough to obscure them completely, but the helicopter didn't seem to see them. The chattering of blades faded away.

Anya unlatched the grate covering the pipe and opened it. The giant O_2 canister worried Jarli. Pure oxygen was explosive. Fortunately, it was only connected to the wall by a small tube. It didn't seem to be part of the air-conditioning system he was about to crawl into.

'I'll give you a boost,' he whispered. He crouched under the open pipe. Without a word, Anya placed one foot on his back, and launched herself up like a gymnast. Jarli looked up in time to see her kicking legs disappear into the pipe. Apparently it was wide enough.

Jarli jumped, grabbed the pipe and scrambled in.

The sharp edge scraped his stomach, but he made it. He found himself in pitch darkness, with steel walls pressed against both his shoulders. He couldn't see Anya. There wasn't enough room to crawl on his hands and knees. He would have to wriggle like a caterpillar through the pipe.

The rumbling of the distant air conditioner was surprisingly loud. Jarli shut his eyes for a moment, fighting off a wave of CLAUSTROPHOBIA. This must have been how Plowman felt inside the car crusher. Right before the walls closed in. *Squish*.

A bright light flashed around the pipe, bouncing off the walls. Anya was using her phone as a torch. Jarli crawled after her, grateful for the light. A cool breeze whistled past him as the big fans sucked in air from outside. He and Anya were moving painfully slowly. Jarli tried not to picture the big truck outside, waiting to pump in the possibly deadly gas. How much time did they have?

Jarli found himself crawling over some wire mesh. He could see through it to the corridor below. The corridor looked empty, but Jarli crossed the mesh as quietly as possible, hoping it would take his weight.

'Corner ahead,' Anya said.

'Great.'

Anya grunted as she wriggled her way around

the sharp bend, then it was Jarli's turn. He managed to squeeze his torso around the corner into the next section of the pipe, but not his legs. His knees didn't bend that way. He was trapped!

'I'm stuck!' he hissed. 'Help!'

'It is OK. Just pull your legs—'

'I can't!' Jarli was panicking now. He couldn't go forward or back. He was going to die here in the dark. Anya couldn't even help him, because there was no room to turn around.

'Listen to me,' Anya said. 'I know it's hard, but you can do it. Just pull your hips through, then roll onto your other side so you can bend your knees. Then keep crawling. Take your time.'

We don't have time, Jarli thought, but he tried. 'It's not working!'

'Keep trying. Grab my ankle, and I'll pull.'

Jarli fumbled around until he found Anya's ankle, then he held on tight. He kept wiggling his hips, trying to get his legs around the bend.

Anya pulled. Jarli kept squirming, his teeth clenched, until—

Finally! His legs were through.

'Thanks,' he gasped.

'No problem. There is a T-intersection up ahead. That should be easier.'

'How will we know which way to go?'

'We will follow the breeze,' Anya said. 'It should lead towards—'

She stopped. Jarli listened. Over the rumbling of the aircon, he could hear something from the corridor below.

Footsteps. Someone was coming.

CRITICAL CONDITION

'OK,' Dr Lanagan said finally. 'I think he's stable.'

Bess glanced at Doug, who looked relieved. The extra transfusions might have saved Plowman's life.

But Taipan's eyes narrowed. 'You *think?*'

'He'll need to be monitored for at least twenty-four hours.' Lanagan switched off the laser scalpel and dropped her tweezers into a bowl with a *clang*. 'And it could take weeks for him to recover completely. But he's out of immediate danger. No thanks to you and your posse showing up, making threats and scaring the wits out of some innocent children. I assume you're leaving now?'

Taipan beamed. 'Excuse me. I need to have a private word with my colleague.'

He and Mamba walked over to the far side of the room and started a quiet conversation. Bess strained to hear what they were saying, but she couldn't make it out.

Doug shuffled over to Bess. 'Why do you think Viper changed his mind?' he whispered.

'About wanting Plowman alive?'

'Yeah.'

'Beats me,' Bess said. 'Mistaken identity, maybe. He might have turned out to be the wrong guy.'

Doug watched the criminals muttering to each other. 'No. They would have just left him. But they were suddenly desperate to save him.'

Bess pulled out her phone.

'Still no signal?' Doug said.

'Yeah. But Jarli's app has a lip-reading function now.' As casually as she could, Bess aimed the camera at the criminals.

Words started appearing on the screen.

>TAKE PLOWMAN WITH US, MAYBE.

>WHAT? WHY?

Bess had actually helped Jarli with this feature of the *Truth* app. She shot video of him talking, and he had done the same to her. Then they had examined the videos without audio, trying to piece together which movements went with which sounds. Lip-reading was surprisingly easy after a bit of practice—although Jarli assured her that turning that skill into workable code had been difficult.

The beta-testing completed, Jarli was now deciding whether or not to release it to the public as a general update. In the right hands it was a useful feature. In the wrong hands it could be dangerous.

>WE CAN'T LEAVE HIM HERE, OR HE'LL HELP THE COPS ID VIPER WHEN HE WAKES UP. BUT WE CAN'T KILL HIM, BECAUSE OF THE WILL. SO TAKING HIM SEEMS LIKE THE ONLY—

>MAYBE NOT. MAYBE VIPER FOUND A WAY TO ERASE THAT INFO FROM SUPPLY CHAIN. THEN IT DOESN'T MATTER WHO HE TALKS TO.

>THAT'S SUPPOSED TO BE IMPOSSIBLE.

>VIPER DOES PLENTY OF IMPOSSIBLE THINGS.

>PLOWMAN'S WILL IS ONLY ACTIVATED IF THE AUTHORITIES KNOW FOR SURE THAT HE'S DEAD, RIGHT?

Now Bess understood what Plowman had been trying to say, before he lost consciousness. *Tell him . . . Will . . .*

It wasn't a name. He had made a will. And learning about it had stopped the criminals from killing him.

They were still talking:

>WHY NOT JUST—

>THERE'S A TRANSMITTER ON HIS HEART. THE WILL IS AUTOMATICALLY ACTIVATED THIRTY SECONDS AFTER HIS HEART STOPS.

>SO... WE TAKE HIM WITH US?

>WE WAIT FOR VIPER. HEY!

Bess heard this last word—because Taipan shouted it. He was looking right at her.

Bess flinched. She locked the phone and tried

to hide it, but it was too late. He stormed over and snatched it out of her hand.

'I was just checking the signal,' she said.

Beep. LIE Her own phone had sold her out. Her heart raced.

'Did you take pictures?' Taipan demanded. 'Video?'

'No,' Bess said.

The app didn't beep, but Taipan still didn't believe her. 'What's your PIN?'

'I didn't take anything,' Bess said. The idea of this psycho going through her phone made her feel ill.

'Mamba,' Taipan said.

Mamba raised her crossbow and pointed it at Bess.

Bess raised her hands. 'Four-five-four-five!' she cried. 'It's four-five-four-five! Don't shoot.'

Taipan unlocked the phone. 'Smart girl,' he said.

Mamba lowered the crossbow.

Taipan swiped back and forth for a while. 'Where are the pictures?'

'I didn't take any.'

Taipan crouched down next to her. His breath smelled like bacon and eggs.

'I'm not going to ask again,' he said.

'I didn't take any pictures!' Bess insisted.

Taipan looked like he was about to say something

else when there was a faint booming sound from overhead. Not thunder. Something closer.

Everyone in the room looked up. The noise had come from the air vent at the top of the theatre, which was covered by a special filter.

There it was again—*boom, thump, clunk*. Distant echoes. It sounded like someone was crawling through the network of air vents.

'Well, well, well,' Taipan said. '*That's* interesting.'

While he was distracted, Bess shuffled away from him, back towards the rest of the group. Hopefully he would forget about her.

'No cop would fit up there,' Mamba was saying. 'Not unless they used to be in the circus.'

'And it's not one of ours,' Taipan said. 'So it must be . . . vermin.' He smiled. 'Shall we call the exterminator?'

Without waiting for a response, he picked up the jammer phone, punched in some numbers, and raised it to his ear.

'Anaconda,' he said. 'We appear to have unwanted guests in our air-conditioning system. We'd be much obliged if you'd . . .'

A pause.

'Excellent,' Taipan said. 'I knew we could count on you.'

BAD VIBRATIONS

Jarli peered down through the grate into the corridor. He saw the man's SHADOW first, and couldn't believe its size—it seemed to darken the whole corridor. The footsteps were so heavy that Jarli felt the vibrations through the walls of the air vent.

'Don't move,' Anya whispered.

Then the man himself came into sight. It took all Jarli's willpower not to scream.

He looked like something out of a fairy-tale. Every part of him was gigantic—his fists, his feet, his head. His bare arms were as long and thick as tree boughs. His hairless brow was so pronounced that his eyes were almost completely hidden.

Stooping to avoid bumping his head on the ceiling, the giant shuffled up the corridor. His clothes looked homemade, or at least home-modified. Extra stitches lined the cuffs of his shirt and his cargo pants.

The giant stopped. He sniffed, looking around. Then he kept moving, clomping away out of sight.

When the footsteps faded, Anya said, 'Who . . . or *what* was that?'

'Anaconda,' Jarli breathed. He remembered seeing something huge, the size of a rhino, rush past when he was partially blinded by the flash grenade. It hadn't even occurred to him that it might be a person.

'How is that even possible?'

'I don't know.' Jarli tried to think of other times he'd seen or heard about people getting that big, but he could only think of comic books. Maybe Anaconda had been exposed to gamma radiation, like the Incredible Hulk.

'I did not see a weapon,' Anya said.

Jarli shuddered. 'He didn't look like he needed one.' The man's hands had been as big as garbage bin lids.

'Well, at least he will not fit in here. Come on.'

They wriggled further up the vent, moving as quietly as possible. Soon they reached the T-intersection, and followed the breeze through the vent.

'Jarli,' Anya whispered. 'We have a problem.'

'That's a nice change.' Jarli tried to see past Anya. It looked like they were at the end of the vent. But a spinning fan was blocking their way.

Anya peered through the blades of the fan at the

room beyond. 'I think that is the control room.'

'Does the fan have an off-switch?'

'Yes, but it's on the other side of the fan.'

'Maybe we can jam it with something.' Jarli looked around. But it was an air vent—nothing here except steel walls and the noise of the turbine.

'I think I could reach through,' Anya said. 'But I would have to be quick.'

Jarli stared at the spinning blades. They were doing at least one rotation per second. 'Don't,' he said. 'They'll cut your hand off.'

'They do not look sharp. At worst, they would break my wrist. And if I time it exactly right—'

'If you break your wrist, how would we get out of here?'

Anya didn't reply.

The blades whipped past, around and around.

'We can backtrack,' Jarli said. It would be hard going backwards, but it seemed like the only option. 'There might be another way down to—'

Anya stuck her hand through the fan.

'Don't!' Jarli hissed.

But it was already over. Anya had snatched her hand back out again, like a snake darting back after a strike.

The whining of the fan became a drone as the blades slowed. Soon they had completely stopped.

Jarli released the breath he'd been holding. 'Still got all your fingers?'

'Eight, nine, ten . . . yes! Piece of cake.'

'That's not funny.'

'Well, comedy is subjective,' Anya said. 'Come on. We have to shut down the rest of the system.' She gripped the blades of the fan and pushed. The whole mechanism swung sideways, and she crawled through.

Jarli followed, gratefully slithering out of the vent into the room beyond. It was cramped and dark, lit only by the LEDs on control panels, but it was nowhere near as stifling as the air vent had been.

A big square machine took up most of the room. It looked like a giant tumble-dryer with fat pipes connecting it to the ceiling. Most of the pipes were metal, but one was made of canvas, like a wind sock. The control panel was huge, with hundreds of buttons and dials, marked with opaque acronyms: **HVAC, ATEX** and **CENELEC.**

'Which button should I press?' Anya said.

Jarli didn't know. He bent down, peering at the underside of the control panel, looking for a power supply. He wished Doug were here. Doug could cut the power to anything, often by mistake.

Something thumped in the corridor outside.

A giant footstep.

Jarli and Anya looked at each other, eyes wide in the gloom. Anya ran over to the narrow door. A simple slide-bolt was screwed into the frame. Anya carefully slid it closed to lock the door.

The bolt made a faint *snick* sound. Immediately, more footsteps echoed through the corridor, getting closer. The giant had heard the sound. And that one tiny bolt wouldn't keep him out for long.

Anya braced her foot against the door, adding her weight to the strength of the bolt.

'Hurry!' she whispered.

Jarli turned back to the control panel. He saw a switch marked **REBOOT**, but that was no good—he needed to stop the aircon system for good. One dial said **FAN SPEED**, so he turned it right down, but he didn't think that would be enough to stop the poison gas.

The doorhandle rattled. Jarli resisted the urge to look behind him.

Suddenly he saw it. A red button in a yellow circle. He couldn't read the words until he wiped the dust off with his thumb.

Jarli pushed the button.

There was a harsh beeping noise. All the lights on the control panel went dead except for a lone standby light. Jarli heard all the turbines in the hospital groan as they wound down. The canvas pipe above the machine deflated and went limp.

Jarli turned to face Anya—

Just in time to see a huge fist punch a hole through the door and grab her.

ILLEGAL OPERATION

The jammer phone rang so suddenly that Bess flinched. Now that her own phone had been taken away, she felt anxious and vulnerable. Which made no sense. Her phone wouldn't have protected her from a crossbow bolt or a grenade, even if it had been working.

Taipan answered the phone. 'Yes, boss.' He snapped his fingers to get Mamba's attention.

Bess held her breath. The criminals had been waiting for further instructions. Now was the moment of truth—would they be ordered to leave? And if they were, would they take Plowman with them?

But when Taipan spoke again, it wasn't what Bess had hoped for.

'Poison gas?' he repeated.

Bess found herself gripping her crutches so tightly that her hands hurt. She looked at Doug, whose eyebrows had disappeared into his blond fringe.

'Of course, boss,' Taipan said. 'I'll tell Anaconda to look for some air-filtration masks.'

Bess doubted that he intended to get enough masks for all the hostages.

Just then, the droning of the aircon faded away to nothing. Bess hadn't even noticed the sound until it was gone. The SILENCE was unnerving.

'Actually,' Taipan said, 'the aircon just stopped. Will that solve the problem?'

There was a pause.

'I see. What are we doing with Plowman?'

Bess could faintly hear the rasping of Viper's voice.

'Brain surgery?' Taipan said. 'I don't understand.'

The two doctors looked alarmed.

Taipan listened for a long time, and then said, 'By phone? Even with instruction, I don't think I can—oh, I see. How do I hook it up?'

Another pause.

'Yes, boss,' Taipan said finally. 'Right away, boss.'

He ended the call.

Lanagan spoke up immediately. 'There's nothing wrong with this patient's brain.'

'That's not your concern,' Taipan said.

'Even if there was, neither of us is a neurosurgeon. We're not qualified to—'

'My boss will do the surgery.' Taipan turned

around to face everybody else in the group. 'Attention please. We're all going to Theatre Two. Move quickly and quietly. Anyone who tries to run will become target practice for my associate.'

Mamba started reloading her crossbow.

Hayes and the kids started shuffling towards the door. But Lanagan and Vorham didn't move.

'Is your boss a qualified neurosurgeon?' Lanagan demanded.

Taipan was pulling a tablet computer out of a satchel. The screen lit up, revealing a picture of a coiled snake. 'Viper is confident that he can perform the operation without killing your patient,' Taipan said. 'He's done it before. You have nothing to worry about. Now, move.'

Lanagan didn't. 'Confidence is not a qualification,' she said. 'And Mr Plowman's brain is fine. I can't allow—'

'I've had enough of you,' Taipan said. 'Mamba?'

Mamba shot Lanagan with the crossbow.

Everyone in the room screamed. Lanagan hit the floor immediately—but Bess noticed that what was sticking out of her leg was not a crossbow bolt. It looked more like a dart, with a feathered tail.

'You can't . . .' Lanagan began. Then her eyes fluttered closed.

Vorham crouched next to her. He ripped out the

dart and sniffed it. 'Is that animal tranquilliser?' he demanded. 'That's not safe for immobilising humans. The dosage—'

'You want to be next?' Mamba asked.

Vorham shut his mouth.

'Don't worry,' Taipan told him. 'We'll switch back to normal crossbow bolts if everyone doesn't get a move on.'

Reluctantly, Vorham lifted Lanagan by the armpits and dragged her out the door. Hayes and the schoolkids followed. Bess looked back in time to see Taipan fiddling with the huge surgical robot. It looked like he was plugging his jammer phone into it.

Maybe the batteries are running low, Bess thought. *Could be an opportunity. If I can just get to it—*

'Move,' Mamba growled.

'OK, OK.' Bess limped out the door.

Mamba herded everyone up the corridor towards the other surgical theatre. No-one tried to flee.

Vorham unlocked the door. Mamba made a threatening gesture with the crossbow, and Vorham handed her the keys.

All the hostages shuffled inside. When someone switched on the lights, Bess saw that Theatre Two was much the same as Theatre One. No surgical robot, but there was an operating table surrounded by blinding lights. A laser scalpel was nearby and a stereo was built into the wall.

Mamba didn't follow them in. Instead, she shut the door and locked it. They were trapped again.

Vorham carried Lanagan over to the operating table. He checked her pulse, her breathing and the dilation of her pupils.

'I think this is an improvement,' Mr Hayes told the students. 'Now we just have to stay calm and wait for the police to intervene.'

'An improvement?' someone said. 'Am I the only one who heard the phrase, "poison gas"?!'

Doug was sitting in the corner, quaking like a dog in a thunderstorm.

Crouching was hard for Bess. She sat next to him instead. 'You OK?' she asked quietly.

Doug didn't even seem to hear her. He was hugging his knees and staring at the wall.

Bess put a hand on his shoulder, and he flinched.

'Don't worry,' she said. 'Like Mr Hayes says, we'll be out of here soon.'

'Didn't you hear?' Doug's voice wavered with fear. 'That guy said *his boss* would be the one performing the surgery.'

It took Bess a moment to realise what this meant.

Viper was coming.

ARMS RACE

The giant's arm was right under Anya's chin, crushing her against the door like the safety bar on a roller coaster. She tried to scream, but couldn't get any air into her lungs. The jagged edges of the hole in the door scraped her back.

She got her hands beneath the arm and tried to bench press it off her chest. It was hopeless. She couldn't move it any more than she could have lifted a truck parked on her torso. It felt like her heart was going to explode.

Jarli ran over, grabbed Anaconda's huge hand, and pulled. But even with their combined strength, they couldn't overpower the giant. Anya was trapped.

'Let me in,' a deep voice snarled from outside. 'Or I'll crush you like a tomato.'

Anya didn't doubt that he could do it. Her ribs were already creaking.

'Hit him,' she wheezed.

'With what?!' Jarli demanded.

'Find something!'

Jarli ran off to search the room for a weapon. But Anya couldn't see one, and soon she couldn't see anything. She was too dizzy. She needed air.

'There's nothing!' Jarli cried.

So Anya did the only thing she could.

She lowered her head and, with the last of her strength, *bit* the arm as hard as she could.

There was a scream of rage from the other side of the door—and the giant's grip loosened. Just for a split second, but it was enough.

Anya slipped out of Anaconda's grip and dropped to the floor. Then she scrambled away from the door just in time, spitting and gagging. The huge hand scrabbled around, but couldn't find her again.

'We gotta get out of here,' Jarli hissed.

Anya was still coughing as the air flooded her lungs. 'The vents,' she choked. 'He won't fit.'

The arm slithered back out the hole in the door. Soon it was replaced by a bloodshot eye under a tremendous brow, peering in at them.

'I'll kill you!' the giant roared.

Jarli was already climbing back into the air vent. As soon as he was in, Anya followed him. It was easier than before. The fear had loosened her joints.

She'd just managed to get her torso in when—

Smash! The door shattered behind her. Footsteps

thudded through the control room towards the vent.

Panicking, Anya wriggled deeper into the vent.

Too slow. A mighty hand grabbed her foot.

Anya thrashed like an eel. Her shoe slipped off, and then she was free, clawing at the floor as she dragged herself towards safety.

The vent shook as Anaconda's arm bashed against the walls, but Anya was out of his reach.

'Anya?' Jarli called from up ahead.

'I'm OK. Keep moving.'

They crawled deeper into the darkness. Anya tried not to listen to the bellows of fury from back in the control room.

Jarli had reached the T-intersection. 'Which way?' he asked.

'Back to the exit,' Anya said. 'We need to tell the cops we shut down the air conditioning. Otherwise they will still gas us.'

'Won't we get arrested?'

'We have bigger problems.' *Literally*, she thought.

Jarli crawled around the corner, heading back the way they had come earlier. Anya suddenly realised that she couldn't hear Anaconda yelling anymore.

'Jarli,' she said. 'Wait.'

Jarli paused. 'What?'

'I think—'

A giant fist punched through the floor of the vent.

Anaconda was in the corridor right beneath them!

The crash was deafening in the confined space. Jarli screamed and scrambled backwards, accidentally kicking Anya in the shoulder. She wriggled back as fast as she could.

The hand, scratched and bleeding from punching through the aluminium, groped around for the two kids. When it couldn't find them, it grabbed the jagged edge of the hole.

Anya saw what was about to happen.

'Get back!' she cried.

But in the confined space, there was no way she or Jarli could move fast enough. There was a screeching, grinding sound as the bolts which connected the air vent to the ceiling were RIPPED out of the concrete. The metal groaned and tore, sheared clean off the ceiling by the strain of holding up the giant's weight. Anaconda had ripped a five-metre-long segment out of the air vent, with Jarli and Anya inside!

For a moment they were trapped in a falling tube, screaming as they bounced weightlessly against the walls and ceiling. Anya covered her face with her arms and—

WHAM! The chunk of the air vent landed in the corridor. Gravity returned with full force, slamming Anya's body against the floor. She felt the ripples in her brain as her skull bounced off her forearms.

Thud, thud, thud. The giant was walking around the fallen segment, trying to work out how to get to the two kids inside.

'What do we do?' Jarli hissed.

Anya's mind was racing. They couldn't hide in here forever. Anaconda was strong enough to rip the metal apart like wrapping paper. They had no weapons to protect themselves, and they couldn't outrun him. By the time they got out of the ruined vent and stood up, he would already be on them.

Suddenly they lurched upwards. Anya screamed. The giant was lifting them into the air!

The metal tube swayed, tilted and shook. Anaconda was trying to tip them out, like a garbage truck emptying a bin.

Anya braced her hands against the sides of the vent, trying not to fall. But her palms were slick with sweat, and the angle was too steep. She slipped down the vent like it was a waterslide and fell out onto the tiled floor of the corridor.

Anya only had a split-second to roll out of the way before Jarli tumbled after her. He stayed down, dizzy. But Anya leapt to her feet and found herself facing the giant.

'You're dead, kid,' he snarled, rubbing the bite mark on his forearm.

With nothing else to do, Anya raised her fists.

It was like stepping into the boxing ring at the gym after school—except that her opponent was more than twice her size. And it wasn't a ring, it was a corridor strewn with rubble. The overhead lights had gone dead. Two chunks of the air shaft were still attached to the ceiling, but they looked wobbly. Maybe she'd get lucky and one would fall on him.

Anaconda didn't raise his fists. Instead, he picked up the fallen chunk of the air vent—a thick steel tube about five metres long. Then he threw it at her.

Anya leapt aside just in time. The metal flew past her and hit the floor down the other end of the corridor, with a sound like crashing cymbals that left Anya's ears ringing. Even after that faded, she could hear an ominous hissing sound.

Now Anaconda threw a punch. Anya ducked. The huge fist whooshed over her head, leaving a vacuum behind it which almost sucked her into its wake.

Anya darted in and struck the giant in the solar plexus. The blow would have left a normal person gasping for breath, but with Anaconda, it was like punching a refrigerator. The impact hurt Anya's hand and jarred her wrist. She darted back. The giant didn't seem at all affected.

He lifted his leg to stomp on her like she was a cockroach. Anya dived out of the way. Anaconda's foot hit the floor so hard that the ground shook.

Anya barely had time to recover before the giant's fist swung down towards her. It was like the sky was falling. She was too slow to get out of the way—

But then Anaconda tripped and went down, face first. Jarli had grabbed his ankle, and was hugging it tightly.

'Run, Anya!' he yelled.

Anya did as she was told, sprinting towards the stairs. Hopefully Jarli was running in the opposite direction. Maybe the giant wouldn't get up in time to catch either of them.

When she reached the stairs, she snatched a look back to check who Anaconda was chasing.

The giant and Jarli both remained on the floor. Facedown, motionless.

Even from this distance, Anya could still hear the hissing sound. She looked at the ripped end of the air shaft, still attached to the ceiling.

The cops didn't know that the aircon system was shut down. They were pumping poison gas into the hospital. Now it was spilling out of the torn-up vent.

And Jarli was breathing it.

RUN LIKE THE WIND

Anya couldn't see or smell the gas from here. But if she inhaled it, she would collapse—fast. Anaconda had gone down immediately, and he was huge.

She took a deep breath and ran back up the corridor. She stepped over the giant, grabbed Jarli's shoulder and shook it. Jarli didn't react. When she lifted his eyelids with her thumbs, his eyeballs had rolled back so only the whites were visible.

Anya couldn't hold her breath much longer. She had to get out of here, fast.

Her lungs burning, she held Jarli by the armpits and dragged him up the corridor. His shoes squeaked across the tiles. He seemed impossibly heavy—the lack of oxygen was already wearing out her muscles.

Keeping her lips clamped shut, she tried to figure out where the gas was. It had knocked Jarli and Anaconda out, and they'd been on the floor, so the gas must be heavier than air. It would be pooling on the floor, an invisible lake of poison. But the aircon wasn't actually pumping, so it wouldn't spread throughout the hospital. Hopefully. Anya just had to get Jarli out of this corridor.

She was already fading. BLACK SPOTS swarmed in from the edges of her vision. *Just lack of oxygen, not poison,* she told herself. But soon she would faint, and end up facedown in the pooling gas. Unable to crawl away before it knocked her out.

Her legs wobbled. There was a rushing noise in her ears, like the raging ocean.

A door swam into view. Anya had no clue where it led, but it looked airtight. If she could get Jarli inside and shut it, maybe they would be safe. At least she would be able to breathe while they planned their next move.

She tried the handle. Unlocked. A rare stroke of luck. The door swung open, hissing like a steam train. Anya dragged Jarli through the gap, and kicked the door closed.

As soon as it shut, the air pressure changed—Anya felt it in her eardrums. The outside world was completely silenced. Finally, she took in a desperate gasp of air.

Not enough. She was still dizzy. She lay on the floor, letting the blood rush to her brain as she took another deep breath. The sparks in her vision winked out one by one. She was going to be OK.

When she could move again, she nudged Jarli.

'Hey. Are you OK?'

Jarli didn't respond.

'Come on. Wake up.' Anya felt Jarli's wrist. His pulse was strong, and it looked like he was breathing. But he wouldn't wake up.

Anya looked around. Maybe she could find some water to splash on him.

The room held several plastic crates, all locked electronically. There was a hose with a shower nozzle, but Anya couldn't find a normal tap—just a button which said **EMERGENCY SPRAY.** Using it might sound an alarm, which could alert the other bad guys.

Suddenly Anya realised where she was. She turned around and around, with growing horror. She was in the hazardous materials room. That was why the door had been airtight, and why all the crates were locked—

Except one.

Anya backed away so fast that she bumped into a wall. One of the crates stood wide open, letting whatever was inside spill into the air.

She forced herself to read the label, to see what she and Jarli had been exposed to.

BOTULISM H.

The deadliest substance in the world, Lanagan had said. *A millionth of a gram could kill everyone in this room by slowly paralysing our bodies, including our hearts and lungs. A litre jug of it would be enough to make the human race extinct.*

And now they were sealed in here with an open box of it.

FMRI

Bang. Bang. Bang. Bang.

'Will you stop that?' Mr Hayes demanded.

Bess kept bashing her crutch against the window. She'd had to climb onto the table to reach, and was wobbling precariously on the other crutch.

She wasn't making any progress. The glass was thick. But maybe it was weakening.

'Even if you break through,' Hayes said, 'We're on the second floor. How would we get down? How would *you* get down?'

Bess gritted her teeth. 'At least I'm doing something. If you've got a better idea . . .' Suddenly she heard voices. She stopped banging on the window, and listened.

'The police will—' Hayes was saying.

'Shh. Listen.' Bess closed her eyes. She wasn't sure why that helped, but it always did. Maybe when she couldn't see, her brain diverted extra power to her ears or something.

Doug ran over. 'What's going on?'

'Just a sec.' Bess clumsily clambered off the table and dragged it over to the wall closest to Theatre One. Then she climbed awkwardly back up.

'*Now* what are you doing?' Hayes asked. 'Get down from there before you hurt yourself.'

Bess ignored him. The voices were louder here. And now she could see why—the stereo was recessed into the wall rather than mounted on it. So the wall was thinner, in just this spot.

Bess pressed her ear to the stereo console.

Mamba's grating voice: 'Don't turn the MRI on yet. Anything magnetic has to be bolted down and moved away.'

'I'm not an idiot,' Taipan sneered.

Thunking and rattling sounds seeped through the wall.

'You think Viper can pull this off?' Mamba asked.

'He's done it before.'

'That was in his own lab, using his own equipment. And we still don't know for sure that it worked.'

'Not our problem,' Taipan said. 'We get paid either way.'

'Oh, really? You think Viper will pay up if Plowman dies?'

'We'll be collecting the money while Viper is doing the surgery. If Plowman dies, it'll be too late to withhold payment.'

'And if he lives?' Mamba grunted. It sounded like she was lifting something heavy.

'Then his will isn't activated. No problem.'

'That's not what I mean. What if Viper lasers the wrong part of his brain, and removes the wrong memories? Then he could still identify all of us when he wakes up.'

'I plan to be long gone by then,' Taipan said.

A visceral shudder ran through Bess's body and she nearly fell off the table. Instantly, Doug was at her feet, ready to catch her.

Removing memories. Was that really possible? The thought of these criminals fiddling around in someone's BRAIN made Bess feel sick.

'You OK?' Doug asked.

'Viper is going to use the laser to fry part of Mr Plowman's brain,' Bess whispered. 'He knows who Viper is, so they're trying to erase his memories.'

Doug looked at Vorham. 'Doctor. Is that possible?'

Vorham looked up from Lanagan. 'Is *what* possible, young man?'

'The bad guys are trying to remove some of Mr Plowman's memories with the laser. Would that work?'

Vorham looked interested. 'Well, brain surgery has come a long way in the last couple of years, using minimally invasive endoscopes instead of bone saws for instance, so . . . perhaps. But every brain stores memories differently. You'd need to wake the patient up and do an fMRI—a kind of brain scan—to see which neurons fire when you make him recall the information. Then you'd need to zap only those neurons with a specialised laser.'

Bess remembered Taipan's tablet computer, and the picture of the snake. He must have been preparing to make Plowman think about Viper, so Viper could remove himself from Plowman's mind.

'But even then,' Vorham continued, 'you'd need an excellent surgeon. Better than anyone in this hospital, frankly.'

'What if the surgeon was just some random criminal?' Doug asked.

'Dead patient,' Vorham said simply. 'Neurosurgeons need about fourteen years of training before they're fully qualified. Brain surgery is not something an amateur can do.'

'What a surprise.'

But they said Viper had done it before, Bess thought. *Which means—*

She didn't have time to finish this thought. There was a thunking, whirring sound from the next room.

'What is *that?*' she wondered aloud.

'The laser scalpel?' asked Doug, his face pale.

'The fMRI,' Vorham said. 'They must be scanning

Mr Plowman's brain and mapping the memory connections.'

The harder Bess tried not to picture the injured man, the more vividly she remembered the image of Plowman's eyes looking into hers. 'How long before they start . . .'

'Minutes, I suspect' Vorham said.

This meant two things.

One: they had run out of time to save Mr Plowman.

Two: Viper was already here.

Bess looked at the doors. They were solid, just like the ones in the other theatre. That had been good news when they were trying to keep the criminals out. Now that the criminals had locked them in, it was bad news. Unless . . .

'Dr Vorham,' she said. 'Does this theatre still have a bone saw?'

CUTTING LOOSE

Sweat poured down Doug's brow as he pushed the bone saw against the door. Splinters and sparks flew as the ultra-sharp blade gouged a hole in the wood.

Doug wasn't quite sure how this had become his job. Vorham was busy looking after Lanagan, but Mr Hayes could have volunteered, instead of 'supervising the other kids'.

Still. Viper was here, so Doug was desperate to be absolutely anywhere else. If this was the fastest way out, so be it.

He was cutting a small semi-circle around the lock. Once he'd finished, they should be able to pull the door right open. But he had to work quickly. At any moment, the criminals could notice the noise or smell of the bone saw and come running.

'Any sign that they've heard us?' Doug grunted.

Bess was standing on the table, listening through the wall, balanced precariously on one crutch. She shook her head and gave Doug a thumbs-up.

Although the MRI machine was still humming

and clanking, there had been no other sounds at all from next door. Doug had expected to hear voices. Maybe the other two criminals were too scared to speak while Viper was concentrating.

Either way, he hoped they were distracted. His bone saw was making a lot of noise.

'Samuel?' Dr Lanagan said.

Doug looked back. Lanagan was awake, staring up at Dr Vorham with dissociative awe.

'Wanda,' Vorham said, holding her hand. Doug hadn't seen much evidence that Vorham felt anything for his patients, or the students in his care. But he showed real warmth towards his colleague.

'How do you feel?' he asked.

Lanagan tried to sit up, but couldn't. 'Like I've been dosed with etorphine hydrochloride,' she said.

'Good guess.'

Doug turned back to his work. It was good that Lanagan was awake. But unless they could get out of this room, none of them would last long.

'Hurry,' Bess urged.

Doug gritted his teeth. 'I'm working as fast as I—'

CRACK! The door fractured, a sudden split running all the way from the top to the bottom. Doug switched off the saw and dumped it on the floor. No point being quiet—there was a strong chance the bad guys had heard the crack. Doug started kicking the door, over and over.

On the fourth kick it smashed wide open with a shower of woodchips.

Doug peered through the doorway. The corridor was empty. So far.

'Come on,' he whispered, and ran towards the stairs. The whole class followed him. Lanagan staggered out last, her arms over the shoulders of Hayes and Vorham.

Doug and Bess reached the stairwell first. Doug started going upstairs, but then he realised Bess was going down.

'Where are you going?' they asked each other at the same moment.

'The roof,' Doug said. 'To get the attention of the police. They could send a helicopter.'

'The bad guys said all the other hospital staff were sealed in the basement,' Bess said. 'We've gotta let them out.'

Doug wished they had discussed this first. 'What's the point of getting them out of the basement, if we can't get them out of the building?'

'We can't just leave them!'

Hayes arrived then. 'Upstairs,' he hissed. 'Quick!'

'There are other hostages in the basement,' Bess insisted.

'It's the police's job to protect them,' Hayes said.

'It's *my* job to protect *you*. Do as I say.'

'You coward!' Bess snapped. 'You're just trying to save yourself.'

Hayes looked stricken. Doug opened his mouth to try to convince Bess—

Then he heard voices from upstairs.

Everyone looked up. Someone was coming down from the roof.

'When will the drone pick up the package?' Mamba was saying.

'Once we put the tracker on it. Viper will want it gone by the time he's finished the surgery,' Taipan replied.

FOOTSTEPS descended towards the students. Doug felt the colour drain from his face. Taipan and Mamba weren't in the surgical theatre with Viper. They had gone up to the roof to drop off a 'package'. Now they were coming back down.

'Downstairs,' he whispered. 'Quick!'

All the students hurried down the stairs. It was impossible for so many people to move silently, especially when two of them—Bess and Lanagan—were limping. But Taipan and Mamba were still talking. They didn't seem to hear their escaping prisoners.

Doug's hand was clammy where it gripped the bannister. With his other hand he held onto Bess, helping her balance.

They reached the ground floor. A big fire door was propped ajar with a brick.

Doug peeked through the gap. Beyond the door was a long corridor, and at the end of it was the front entrance to the hospital. A big, tough-looking woman with broad shoulders and fingerless gloves stood there, a gleaming cutlass holstered on her hip.

'What's going on?' Bess whispered.

'The front door is guarded,' Doug replied. He was just trying to work out how to sneak past the swordswoman when there was a yell from upstairs.

'Taipan—the kids are gone!'

'What?!'

The criminals had seen the smashed door. Footsteps approached the stairwell.

'The doctors, too,' Mamba growled. 'And the teacher.'

'Search the building! Find them!'

Doug and Bess looked at each other. 'The basement,' Bess hissed. 'Hurry!'

She was right. It was the only way. Doug scrambled down the stairs, followed by everyone else. The air was colder with every step. They were getting deeper and deeper underground.

Finally they reached the bottom, where there was another fire door. It had no lock, but a thick wooden mop lay on the floor, wedged between the door and the opposite wall. Both ends of the mop were fixed in place with duct tape. Anyone pushing from the other side would have no hope of getting through.

Someone was coming down the stairs. Either Taipan or Mamba. Doug grabbed the mop and pulled with all his might, ripping the tape free. He chucked the mop aside and pulled open the fire door.

Beyond was a dark, ugly room with a furnace on one side and a row of open-topped cages on the other. The cages were brimming over with stained sheets. Eight or nine people were huddled in the corners of the room—some old people in hospital gowns, a woman in a lab coat, two nurses in scrubs and a uniformed paramedic.

'Oh, thank God!' someone said. A beak-nosed man in nurse's scrubs.

'Is Tyson with you?' the paramedic asked.

Doug ran through, followed by the schoolkids. He waited until Hayes and Vorham had carried Lanagan through before he slammed the door.

'What are you doing?' the nurse cried. His nametag said **AMON.**

'Is there another way out of here?' Doug demanded.

'Why would we still be here if there was?'

Fair point. 'OK, then we need to seal this door.'

'We've been trying to get it open for more than an hour!'

'The bad guys are right behind us. Please, just—'

Too late. The door burst open, hitting Doug in the back of the head. He stumbled forward, eyes watering. Mamba rushed in, brandishing her crossbow.

Everyone stuck their hands up.

Mamba looked around the room at all the terrified faces. It took Doug a moment to realise she was doing a headcount.

'Problem solved,' she called over her shoulder. Then she backed out of the room and slammed the door. Doug heard her fiddle around outside until the mop was back in place.

They were locked in.

CONTAGION

'Do you remember what the doctor said about botulism H?' Jarli asked.

'Vividly.' Anya was sitting on the floor, her head hanging low. 'In particular, I remember the bit about a litre jug of it making humanity extinct.'

Yeah. Jarli remembered that part too.

They were in the airlock between the corridor and the hazardous materials room. They couldn't go back out into the corridor because of the gas, and they couldn't go into the hazmat room because of the open botulism box. They were trapped in about four square metres of floor space with glass on one side. It was like being in a fish tank.

The door to the hazmat room was shut. According to Anya, it had been ajar when she dragged Jarli into the airlock. She had closed it immediately, but the botulism box could have been open for hours, leaking dangerous particles into the air. They had almost definitely been exposed.

Anya had said all this with grim certainty, but

she said most things with grim certainty. Jarli was sure there was hope.

'This is a research hospital,' he said. 'They were working on a cure, right?'

'Yes,' Anya said. 'But they hadn't found one yet, or else they would have destroyed the samples.'

'Maybe they did destroy them.' Jarli peered through the glass. 'That sure looks like an empty box to me.'

'Botulism is made by microscopic bacteria. The particles would be too small to see.'

'But then why was the door unlocked? Why was the airlock open?'

Anya shrugged. 'I don't know.' She wouldn't meet his gaze. Shc hadn't looked at him once since confirming that he was alive and unharmed.

'This isn't your fault,' Jarli said. 'You know that, right?'

'I dragged you in here,' Anya said.

'If you hadn't, we would both be unconscious and breathing poison gas right now.'

'But not dying, probably,' Anya said.

'We're not dying. I feel fine.' Jarli stood up, and immediately wobbled. He was still a bit woozy from the gas.

Anya's phone beeped. LIE

Lanagan had said the toxin would paralyse them.

Jarli could still feel all his fingers and toes. Would they go NUMB when the botulism started to take effect? Or would he still be able to feel everything as his muscles went slack, one by one?

He had a sudden flash of his parents seeing him through the glass, here in this airlock, his body frozen on the floor.

His parents had been acting strange lately, particularly his father. It was as if they thought Jarli was up to something. That hadn't seemed to matter this morning—Jarli had thought he'd have plenty of time to get back in their good books. Now he might never see them again.

Blinking away tears, he paced back and forth in the airlock. 'We *might* not have been exposed,' he said. 'We've gotta get to a doctor who can examine us.'

'We cannot leave.'

'If we hold our breath—'

'We cannot leave,' Anya said again. 'What if the disease is contagious? I do not want to accidentally make humanity extinct. Do you?'

Jarli hesitated. That *would* be bad.

His eyes settled on the hazmat suits. There were two of them, hanging from hooks on the airlock wall. 'Do you think those would fit us?'

'We have already been exposed,' Anya said.

'*Maybe*. But they could protect us from the gas, and they could stop us from exposing anybody else.'

Anya looked at the suits for a minute. Eventually she said, 'How much air do you think is in those tanks?'

Jarli peered at the tube on the side. 'Six point eight litres, apparently.'

'How long would that last? Assuming it is full. Which it probably is not, since we just saw some people using them when we arrived.'

Jarli shrugged. 'Dunno. I've never been scuba diving. But it would be long enough to get us out of here, right?'

'We will not fit through the air ducts with those suits on.'

'We don't have to. There are doctors held hostage right here in the hospital. We just have to find them.'

Anya didn't look convinced. 'They will be guarded, surely.'

Jarli threw up his hands. 'Well, either we give it a shot, or we sit here waiting to die. Which would you prefer?'

'Alright,' Anya said finally. 'Let's try the suits.'

It took fifteen minutes just to get the suits on. They had special airtight zips at the back like the kind on a bag of dog food—Jarli and Anya had to help each other get zipped up. The crinkly plastic sleeves were heavier than they looked. The helmets were designed to be screwed on. Jarli had to turn his around and around several times before it was tight.

When he got the visor facing the right way, it lit up with a special heads-up display. Most of the numbers meant nothing to Jarli, but he quickly found the important bit: 61 MINUTES AIR REMAINING (APPROX).

Would that be enough? Jarli had to hope so.

'How much air do you have?' he asked Anya. His own voice seemed deafening inside the helmet. There was a faint hissing as his breaths were sucked out and fresh air pumped in from the tank.

'Sixty-four minutes,' Anya said, her voice muffled by the suit.

'Plenty,' Jarli said. 'Let's do this.'

PART THREE: ESCAPE

'AN UNINTENDED SIDE-EFFECT—THE APP MAKES IT DIFFICULT FOR THE *USER* TO LIE. IF YOU'RE FOCUSED ON THE APP, IT'S HARD TO COME UP WITH A PLAUSIBLE STORY AND GAUGE WHETHER THE OTHER PERSON BELIEVES YOU. BUT I'M NOT INTERESTED IN FIXING THAT BUG, BECAUSE IT'S EASY TO AVOID. JUST TELL THE TRUTH, PEOPLE.'

—From the documentation for Truth, *version 4.3*

HELL OR HIGH WATER

Doug was walking around the perimeter of the room, knocking on the red brick walls.

'There's no way out of here,' said the nurse—he'd introduced himself as Amon. 'We checked.'

'No harm in checking again,' Doug said. The bricks were really cold. There was probably dirt on the other side. So deep, so tightly packed, that the sun's warmth never seeped down to it.

'You should save your energy,' Amon said.

'For what?' Doug asked.

'As you may have noticed, there's no food down here.'

Some of the other hostages grumbled quietly. They were sitting on the floor, leaning against walls and cages. There wasn't enough room down here for twenty people.

Doug had heard of the rule of three: a human being could survive three minutes without air, three hours without heat, three days without water, three weeks without food. But he'd eaten lunch only six hours ago and he was already hungry again.

'What if the siege goes on for weeks?' Amon was saying. 'That's not unheard of.'

Mr Hayes patted the air—a *settle down* gesture. 'The police must be here by now,' he said. 'Nobody panic. I'm sure we'll be out of here soon.'

Doug wasn't willing to wait. Viper, the monster, the big boss, was right upstairs. They had to get out of here *now*.

'What about water?' he asked Amon.

Amon gestured to a sink in the opposite corner. 'Go nuts,' he said.

Doug walked over to the sink. It was a deep trough, maybe designed for rinsing bedsheets. He turned a squeaky tap, cupped his hands under the flow of cold water and took a few sips.

As he turned off the tap he examined the sink. He had hoped that maybe the drain would be big enough to escape through, but it was no wider than his hand, and the pipe beyond equally small. They couldn't get out that way.

There was a power point nearby. Could he use electricity to burn through the door somehow? Unlikely. And dangerous, especially given the flammable cladding in the walls which Lanagan had mentioned.

Doug turned the problem over and over in his

mind. He was good with mechanical problems. His mother always said that he understood absolutely anything with wheels. 'And nothing without them,' she would add, when she thought he wasn't listening.

We could block the drain, Doug thought. *Flood the trough. Fill this whole room with water. Then what would happen?*

Well, the hostages would float to the ceiling. What was up there?

Doug looked up. Nothing useful. A few more small pipes. Two ventilation grills, each about the size of pencil cases. Too small to escape through.

But water was *heavy*. Doug did some quick maths. The room was about five metres wide, eight deep, three high. That was . . . a hundred and twenty cubic metres of space. A cubic metre was a thousand litres, a litre of water weighed a kilogram, a thousand kilograms was a tonne.

Doug walked back over to the fire door. It was wooden. Strong enough to resist a kick. But could the mop outside support a hundred and twenty tonnes of water? Surely not. It would snap, the door would break open and they would be free.

First problem: it would take a long time. Doug visualised himself filling a litre jug from the tap. How long would that take? Say five seconds. Which meant that filling the whole room would take . . .

six hundred thousand seconds. Ten thousand minutes. One hundred and sixty-six hours. The last calculation—one hundred and sixty-six divided by twenty-four—was too hard to do precisely in his head, but he figured it was about a week.

Second problem: depending on how the pump worked, the water might stop flowing when they were only neck deep.

Third problem: even if he could get the water flowing faster somehow, and guarantee that it didn't stop, he was pretty sure the patients in here would be too weak to swim.

Maybe they could build a raft out of something. He looked around for buoyant materials. But everything in here was made of brick or iron.

He turned to Bess and opened his mouth to ask how well she could swim. But she spoke first.

'Are you thinking what I'm thinking?' she asked.

Doug hesitated. 'Uh . . . maybe.'

Bess turned to Amon. 'That's the furnace, right?'

She was pointing at a huge iron box built into the wall. There was a rusty grate on the front.

'The incinerator,' Amon said. 'Some things can't be reused, and are too contagious to just throw away. We have to burn them.'

'So where's the chimney?'

Amon hesitated. 'I don't know.'

'There must be one,' Bess said. 'Those little air vents up there wouldn't be enough to clear the smoke.'

'I guess it's behind the wall,' Amon said. 'It would get pretty hot. They wouldn't want to risk someone touching it.'

'How wide is it?'

Amon raised his eyebrows. 'The chimney? I don't know. I've never been up on the roof.'

Doug liked the sound of this plan. Climbing a chimney might be difficult, but it would be better than treading water for a week.

'I'll check it out,' he said, approaching the incinerator.

'Doug,' Hayes said. 'I don't think this is a good idea.'

'I'm just taking a look.' Doug opened the grate to expose the inside of the incinerator. A row of rolling cylinders lined the floor, so things could easily slide in. Ash carpeted the floor beneath them.

He pushed his head and shoulders right in. The incinerator was cold, but it smelled like a campfire. It was deeper than it had looked from the outside, which meant that a section of it was behind the wall. He couldn't see a chimney. But with his shoulders blocking the light, he couldn't see much of anything.

He pulled his phone out of his pocket and brought

up a torch app. He shone the light around the inside of the incinerator. The walls were charred black by thousands of fires, so it was still hard to see.

But there *was* a chimney in the low ceiling. It was square, about as wide across as Doug's desk at school. It wouldn't be comfortable, but he could fit.

Actually *climbing* it would be another matter.

He wriggled backwards out of the incinerator. 'It's possible,' he said. 'I think.'

'It might be possible for a fourteen year-old kid,' Amon said. 'But there's no way the adults will fit.'

'They don't have to,' Bess pointed out. 'If one person can climb up to the roof, then they can come down the stairs and let the rest of us out.'

'And then what?' Hayes said. 'The exit is guarded. We're safest if we stay here and wait for the police.'

'Why do you think the police haven't come in yet?' Bess snapped. 'It's because they know the bad guys have hostages. If we hide somewhere else in the building, and the bad guys don't know where we are, then the police can come in safely.'

'And how are they supposed to know that we're in hiding?'

'Because Doug can signal them when he's on the roof, and tell them about the plan ahead of time. Right, Doug?'

Privately, Doug wondered how he could tell the

police anything. Would they hear him, shouting from the rooftop? But it seemed like the least doubtful part of this plan, so he nodded.

'Well, that's settled,' Bess said.

'No, it isn't,' Hayes said.

But Doug was already crawling into the incinerator.

'Good luck,' Bess called.

Doug didn't respond. If he opened his mouth, he was pretty sure it would fill up with ash.

He wriggled along the rolling cylinders towards the back of the incinerator. It was wide and long enough for a human being, and he couldn't help but wonder if the hospital used it to cremate bodies. If someone died here and they had no family to collect them, the hospital would need to get rid of them somehow.

This made Doug think about his own family. His mum and dad must know about the crisis by now. They would be really scared. Dad didn't handle stress well. And if Doug died, they would be so mad at him.

He decided not to die.

The chimney didn't go straight up—it twisted back and forth, forcing Doug to contort his body into uncomfortable shapes. He bumped his head a couple of times as he crawled upwards, feeling the shape of the chimney as he went.

Soon his hands found a thin wire mesh blocking the tunnel. It felt like a fly screen. It was probably supposed to stop dangerous particles from shooting up the chimney and pouring out into the atmosphere. All this dust was probably TOXIC. Doug couldn't wait to get home and have a shower.

The mesh wasn't very strong. Doug jabbed his finger through it, then ripped it wide open with his hands and crawled through.

'You OK in there?' someone called. Hayes, or Amon—the echoes made it hard to tell.

Doug still wasn't willing to open his mouth. He rapped his knuckles on the iron wall twice instead—*tong, tong*.

The rest of the chimney was directly above him now, going straight up. He could see a tiny speck of light at the very top—even the night sky was brighter than this pitch-black tunnel. There was no ladder, and no handholds. But the gritty walls felt like sandpaper. If he pressed his hands against the wall on one side and his back against the other, he wouldn't fall.

He started climbing, inch by inch, wedged between the walls. It was like crawling on his hands and knees, but upwards. A funny thought struck him—*this must be how Santa feels, climbing chimneys*. The image was so ridiculous that a burst of hysterical laughter almost bubbled up out of his throat. He swallowed it back down and kept climbing.

Once he was a couple of metres up, the burnt-toast smell didn't seem so bad. Maybe the worst gases lingered near the incinerator. Or maybe his nose was getting used to it.

Doug's arms were already starting to tremble from the strain of supporting his body. *Take it easy,* he told himself. *Three metres up*—it was just a guess—*and only fifteen or twenty to go*.

Another laugh threatened to dislodge him. He was losing his mind in here.

And then he heard something from down below. A rattle and a clank.

The door to the basement was opening.

FEE FI FO FUM

When Jarli and Anya got back to the corridor with the destroyed air vent, they were alarmed to see that it was empty. The sleeping giant had disappeared.

Jarli blinked, turning around and around. It seemed impossible that something so big was just gone.

'Maybe his friends came and found him,' Jarli whispered.

'How would they carry him? He was as big as an elephant. And anyway, the gas would have knocked them out too.'

'So you reckon he woke up?'

'I think we have to assume that,' Anya said, her voice muffled by the helmet.

'At least that means the gas has gone.' Jarli started fiddling with his helmet.

Anya grabbed his arm. 'Wait. We do not want to infect anybody else with botulism. And even if there is not enough poison gas in the air to sedate a giant, you or I may not be so lucky.'

'You're so negative,' Jarli muttered. He looked around for footprints. There were none. They couldn't be sure which way Anaconda had gone.

'The plan is unchanged,' Anya said. 'We need to find the doctors.'

'Let's try the surgical theatres,' Jarli suggested. 'That's where they were going before the bad guys showed up. Maybe we can find out where they went.'

He followed Anya through the winding corridors of the hospital. They paused to peek around every corner, wary of the giant. Jarli's helmet was freaking him out. He couldn't hear properly, and the visor wasn't wide enough—he had no peripheral vision. He couldn't shake the feeling that Anaconda was sneaking up on them. And the tough plastic made it hard to move quickly or quietly. If they were spotted, they wouldn't be able to outrun the criminals.

Finally they reached the first theatre. The door had been smashed open. Pieces of it lay all over the corridor.

'Looks like the bad guys got in,' Jarli whispered.

'Someone broke *out*,' Anya said. 'The pieces are in the corridor, not the room.'

They peeked through the doorway. The theatre looked empty. A table had been dragged across the room to a different wall. No blood anywhere.

'Hello?' Jarli called. 'It's us!'

'Anya and Jarli,' Anya added.

No response. No-one was hiding in here.

'Let's try the other one,' Anya said.

They shuffled over to Theatre Two and tried the door. Locked.

Jarli could hear SOUNDS from inside. Humming, clicking, whirring. Mechanical sounds, but not repetitive. Not random, either. And the steady *beep, beep, beep* of a heart monitor. The sounds of an operation in progress.

Jarli knocked on the door.

The sounds continued.

Jarli knocked again, louder. 'Hey! It's just us. Let us in!'

For about twenty seconds, there was no sign that whoever was inside had heard him. Jarli was about to try again when the strange noises stopped. All but the beeping of a heart.

Jarli waited for someone to call out, or open the door. But no-one did.

The room wasn't empty. If it was his friends in there, or other hostages, Jarli felt sure that they would say something. But no-one did.

So someone else was in there. Doing surgery.

Anya and Jarli both backed away from the door. Jarli wasn't quite sure what was going on, but he knew it wasn't good.

'This way,' Anya hissed. They ran towards the stairs. But as they got closer, Jarli heard someone coming up from the ground floor.

He grabbed Anya. 'No! Go back.'

They hurried back up the corridor and ducked through the smashed door into Theatre One. Once they were inside, they hid behind the operating table.

They waited for a long time. No-one passed by the corridor outside. Jarli didn't hear the doors to Theatre Two opening. Whoever was doing the surgery, they had decided to ignore the knocking.

'What do we do now?' he whispered.

'Keep searching, I suppose. The doctors must be somewhere else.'

'But so are the bad guys. And we only have thirty minutes of air left in these suits.'

'You have a better idea?' Anya asked.

'Yes.' Jarli said. He ran over to the laser scalpel. It wasn't the same one Doug had been told not to touch, but it looked identical. The trolley had a control panel mounted on it. The buttons all lit up when Jarli twisted a key which had been left in the ignition.

Anya looked alarmed. 'What are you suggesting exactly?'

'Just a sec,' Jarli said. The handle, which looked

like a price check gun, was mounted on a mechanical arm. Jarli swivelled it, taking aim at the floor. Then he found the LASER ON switch and pushed it.

A bright blue dot appeared, but not on the floor. It appeared on a ceramic tile mounted in front of the laser. That must be a safety feature, to stop people from accidentally cutting their fingers off. Jarli tried to work out how to move the tile out of the way.

'What are you doing?' Anya demanded.

Jarli found the RELEASE SAFETY button and pushed it. The tile slid aside, and the bright dot of the laser appeared on the floor. A spiral of smoke immediately corkscrewed out of it.

'Getting us out of here,' Jarli said. Then he swivelled the laser to face the window.

The air filled with crackling and hissing as the thick glass began to melt.

INFERNAL DEVICES

Hostages scrambled away from the door as it opened. Taipan strolled in first, holding a grenade and leering.

'No sudden movements,' he said. 'In an enclosed space like this, a flash grenade can kill.'

Mamba came in after him, crossbow raised. She said nothing.

Bess resisted the temptation to look at the incinerator. Had the criminals heard Doug in the chimney? Did they realise an escape attempt was underway?

If they did, they showed no sign. Mamba levelled her crossbow at Hayes and Amon, who were sitting down near the far wall.

'Everybody up,' she said. 'We're doing some digging down here—we need you out.'

Bess cleared her throat. 'Where are we going?'

Mamba swivelled to face her. 'No questions,' she said.

Bess raised her hands. 'OK, OK.'

Mamba stepped aside and pointed at the door. Everyone shuffled slowly towards it, sneaking anxious glances at each other.

'Wait,' Mamba said.

Everyone stopped.

'What is it?' Taipan asked.

Mamba swept her gaze across the terrified hostages. 'We're short.'

Bess could feel her heart pumping faster and faster.

Taipan's eyes narrowed. 'You're certain?'

'Yes. One's missing.'

Taipan started looking around the room for escape routes, just as Doug had been doing earlier.

'You must have counted wrong,' Bess said.

Several phones in the room beeped. LIE

Bess cursed Jarli and his stupid app.

'Nice try,' Taipan said. 'Tell me where—'

His gaze settled on the incinerator with the open grate.

'Never mind,' he said.

'We were just looking,' Bess said.

Beep. LIE

Taipan leaned down, inspecting the inside of the incinerator. Bess had done the same thing a minute ago, and Doug's feet hadn't been visible. Hopefully he would keep quiet.

'No sign of anyone,' Taipan said finally. 'I apologise for doubting you, young lady.'

But he was grinning. His expression made Bess uneasy.

She shrugged. 'Um, no problem.'

'Mamba must have miscounted,' Taipan said.

Beep. LIE

Mamba raised an eyebrow.

'Everybody out, please,' Taipan said. 'Follow Mamba up the stairs.'

As the hostages started to shuffle out, Taipan closed the grate—

Then he touched a button on top of the incinerator.

The button was marked IGNITION.

'No!' Bess screamed.

There was a click, and then a hiss.

The flame ignited.

At first, Doug wasn't sure what the sounds meant. Clunking, gasping . . .

And then he heard a horrifying *whumpf*. It sounded just like the barbeque at home. It was the sound of gas catching fire.

No, he thought. *No, no, no!*

A faint glow flickered beneath him. The fire was

about ten metres below, but already the heat was starting to cook the soles of his shoes. The metal walls were heating up against his palms.

If he stayed here, he would be roasted like a chicken. And if he fell . . .

Doug started climbing again, faster this time. He didn't care about moving quietly anymore. He only wanted to get away from those flames, fast.

Plumes of smoke swept up the chimney past him, blocking out the light above. He choked on the bitter air, his eyes watering and his nose running. If he didn't get out of here soon, the smoke would suffocate him. *Three minutes without air.* Then he would fall into the fire below.

He crawled upwards in a blind panic, coughing and trembling. His sweaty hands made the metal slippery. It was hard to hold on. The fabric of his trousers felt searing hot against his skin. If his pants ignited, he was doomed.

The flames didn't just crackle—they *roared*. Like a cyclone, or a jet engine. If he screamed, no-one would hear it. Hot wind whipped past him as he climbed. Flakes of ash stung his face.

Then his head bumped into something. A roof.

Doug did scream, then. There was a lid on the chimney! He was trapped! He was going to die—

No. Not a lid. Another mesh, to stop particles

escaping into the atmosphere.

Bracing one quivering arm against the wall, Doug frantically tore at the mesh with his other hand. The thin wires were so hot that they had started to glow red. When his hand eventually punched through, the shredded ends scratched his skin like broken glass. Ignoring the pain, Doug ripped up the mesh and scrambled further upwards.

Air. Moist, silky air on his face. With the last of his strength, he dragged himself out of the chimney and tumbled onto the roof. Raindrops spattered his face. The first stars were coming out. The concrete under his back was cold and sandy. For a moment it felt like being back home, lying on the riverbank and watching the lights of the city come on.

Too giddy to stand, he turned his head to survey the roof. There was a radio antenna, a couple of aircon units, a wooden crate and a door to the stairwell. He should go back down to the basement and let the others out.

But what was he supposed to do first? Doug struggled to remember the plan. The smoke was clouding his mind.

Oh yeah. Communicate with the police . . . somehow. He wondered if the jammer would still be on.

Doug sat up and waited for the world to stop

spinning. He pulled his phone out of his pocket and dropped it with a yelp—it was too hot to handle.

He wrapped his hands in his ashen shirt and pushed the power button. The screen wouldn't light up. The phone was cooked. Doug's battery often overheated just trying to run graphics-heavy games. Now it was well and truly dead.

He would have to shout. His vocal cords felt shredded, but hopefully he would be able to get the attention of the police below. If they were here.

Doug was about to crawl over to the edge of the rooftop when he heard something. From the stairwell. Someone was coming.

'Oh, *come on!*' he groaned. Could he have just a little bit of good luck, for once?

None of the aircon units were big enough to hide behind, and he wasn't sure he would be able to reach them anyway. His arms and legs were still so weak after the climb. The only useful thing nearby was the wooden crate.

He dragged himself over to it. It was big enough to hide behind, but that wouldn't help if the criminals searched the roof.

The crate was sealed with duct tape. Doug pulled out his keys and quickly sawed through the tape. Then he lifted the lid and climbed into the crate.

It wasn't quite empty. There was a large vacuum

flask, the kind used for soup, nestled in a bed of polystyrene at the bottom. But there was still enough room for Doug. Hopefully from outside, the crate wouldn't look like it had been tampered with. He had sliced the tape pretty cleanly. The damage shouldn't be obvious unless they got very close.

Unfortunately, it sounded like they were getting closer.

Footsteps thumped across the rooftop towards the box. Taipan? Mamba? Someone else? It was impossible to tell. There were no voices. Doug held his breath.

The footsteps got closer and closer, until—

Thunk. Something hit the side of the box. *Beep*.

It sounded like someone had attached something to the outside of the crate. Something electronic. A bomb? A cutting tool? Doug's scalp prickled with sweat.

The footsteps receded, and then paused.

With no clue what was happening outside, Doug lay perfectly still. With all the ash in his hair and on his clothes, he probably looked like a rock. If they lifted the lid, they might not even realise he was human.

Another sound filled the air. A buzzing, whirring sound that Doug knew well.

A DRONE. A big one, it sounded like.

Too late, Doug remembered the fragment of conversation he'd overheard between Taipan and Mamba:

When will the drones pick up the package?

Once we put the tracker on it. Viper will want it gone by the time he's finished the surgery.

Doug tried to sit up, but—

Clunk! Clunk! Metal claws latched onto the sides of the crate. It lurched up into the air so suddenly that Doug slipped over and fell back into the polystyrene bedding.

Terror seized his heart. He had made the crate twice as heavy by climbing inside. What if the drone couldn't carry it? What if the claws released it as the drone flew over the hospital grounds, leaving Doug screaming inside as he plummeted towards certain death?

But apparently the drone was strong enough. The crate soared up and away towards Viper's hideout, with Doug trapped inside.

PLAN B

'Move,' Mamba said, shoving Bess' back.

Bess stumbled, but didn't fall. It seemed impossible that she was still upright, plodding along with a crossbow pointed at her back, while Doug was dead. Just ashes, floating out of the chimney.

Because of her. It had been her dumb idea which got him killed. If it weren't for her, Doug would be marching along this corridor with them.

Mr Hayes took Bess's hand, keeping her upright. 'Hey. You OK?'

His concern only made her feel worse. 'No.' She kept her voice low so Mamba couldn't hear them. 'I'm a long way from OK.'

She half-expected him to chide her for weakness. Or blame her for convincing Doug to climb that chimney. But he didn't.

'I know this is scary,' Hayes said. 'For everyone. But it'll be over soon—you just have to keep it together a little longer. Alright?'

He was wrong. It wasn't scary. Doug's voice in her

head: *Hard to be scared when the worst has already happened*. The fear had faded, leaving behind only a sense of hopelessness.

'They're going to kill us all,' Bess said.

'I won't let that happen,' Hayes promised.

He sounded completely genuine, and no-one's phone beeped. But with Doug dead, Bess didn't trust him to save the rest of them.

'No more talking,' Mamba growled.

They trudged through the doors to the main foyer, where they had entered the hospital a lifetime ago. The woman with the sword was here, her face like a bronze statue.

Taipan closed the doors behind them, sealing them in the foyer. Bess didn't see him lock the doors, although she doubted that mattered. Even if the hostages somehow got the chance to run, there was nowhere to go.

'All yours, Rattler,' Taipan said. He was tossing a grenade from hand to hand again. 'I'll tell Anaconda to start digging.'

'Alright,' the woman with the sword said. She turned to the hostages. 'Listen up.'

Bess had kind of thought she would talk like a pirate, because of the sword, but she didn't. She had some other kind of accent, maybe American.

'I want everybody to sit still on the floor, over

there.' Rattler pointed. 'Near the doors.'

'Why?' someone asked.

'What was that?' Rattler drew her sword. *Shing*.

The question was not repeated.

Everyone—students, doctors, nurses, Mr Hayes—shuffled over to the glass doors. They were locked. Bess found a space, laid her crutches down and leaned against the window.

There were more police cars outside than she had ever seen in Kelton. Swirling lights threw flashes of blue and red across the hillside, bouncing off the clouds in the night sky. Police huddled in the shadows behind vehicles. There were plenty of cops, but if they stormed in, they would have to trample through all the kids to get to the criminals.

That's why Rattler made us sit here, Bess realised. The thought that she was being used as a human shield filled her with RAGE.

Down the hill a little further there was a temporary fence where more police were keeping reporters back. And not just reporters—parents. Bess could see a row of horrified faces, pale and tear-streaked in the beams from the floodlights. She looked for her own parents but couldn't see them in the crowd.

But she saw a few familiar faces. Jarli's mum, clinging to the fence, her hair a mess, her eyes wide. Jarli's dad, hulking and grim. There was a man with dark circles around his eyes—Bess knew him as Scanner. He was a police officer who had been undercover in Viper's organisation for months. He had saved Jarli's life once. Bess would have been reassured to see him, except that he looked just as worried as all the parents around him.

She saw Doug's mum and dad, too. They looked frightened rather than grief-stricken. They didn't know he was dead. Tears brimmed over in Bess's eyes. She wiped them away with her sleeve.

'Hey! Cripple! I said don't move.'

Bess gritted her teeth, and put her palms back in her lap. She could see the reflection of the criminals, who were having a discussion behind her, on the opposite side of the foyer. Without using the app, it was hard to read their lips. But she saw a word, or thought she did:

Tunnel.

There was a network of old coal mining tunnels under Kelton. Bess had been down there once. Maybe one of them ran under the hospital, and that was why the criminals wanted the hostages out of the basement.

They were planning their escape.

CROWD CONTROL

'Move aside,' Constable Blanco shouted. 'I'm a police officer. Make way!'

She brandished her wallet. Her badge had been taken away when she was suspended, so she was actually flashing her driver's license at people. It was dark and she figured no-one would look too closely.

Unfortunately, people didn't move out of her way. They rushed inwards instead. Blanco found herself crushed in a scrum of desperate parents and eager reporters. They looked wild. The rain had drenched everyone, leaving hair frizzy and make-up running.

'Whose drone was that taking off from the roof?' someone demanded. 'Was that you guys?'

'My daughter is in there!' someone else cried. 'Her name is Anya. Please, I need—'

'Can you comment on the rumours that the crime lord known as Viper is—'

'Please help us, our son—'

Blanco turned her head away as a reporter's flash went off, momentarily blinding her. She had a very bad feeling about this. With so many worried parents out here, the school group must still be inside. She'd called Arno as soon as she'd received the message from Jarli about the attack on the hospital. But when she'd tried to call the boy back, he hadn't answered. She hadn't been able to find him at his house or in town either. Was he being held hostage too?

'Get back, everyone,' Blanco snarled, barging people aside. The deep puddles soaked through her shoes. If anyone fell over and got trampled, they could actually drown.

'Tell us about the drone!' someone yelled.

'My husband's name is Henry Hayes,' a woman said. 'He's in there. Please—'

As Blanco pushed through the crowd, she pictured the timeline on the wall in her study.

Wednesday 4:32pm

An email from witness 0 claiming suspect 5 has told him Viper's identity. We plan to meet the next day.

Thursday 9:17am

Witness 0 never shows. Doesn't answer his phone or respond to my messages. He seems to have dropped off the face of the earth.

Friday 1:30pm

Police pull suspect 5 out of a car crusher and rush him to hospital.

Friday 2:30pm

Viper stages an elaborate distraction at a factory on the other side of town and escapes.

Friday 3:53pm

Police discover armed criminals have taken over the hospital, trapping suspect 5 and witness 0 inside.

None of this was good, but the worst part was that the only two people who knew Viper's identity—or claimed to—were both in grave danger. The whole situation was spinning out of control.

She reached the temporary fence and the police officers beyond. One of them was a face she recognised.

'Rodney!' she shouted. 'Hey! Rodney!'

Rodney spun around, and scanned the faces in the crowd on the other side of the fence. He spotted Blanco quickly, and came closer to the fence.

'Let me through,' Blanco said. 'Quick.'

'You know I can't do that,' Rodney said.

Blanco could feel the people around her starting to take notice of the conversation. 'This is Viper again, isn't it?' she said. 'He distracted you on the other side of town so he could do something here. You need all the help you can get.'

'We're about to move in. We don't have time for more theories.' Rodney turned away.

'Wait,' Blanco said. 'I have a witness who says he can identify Viper.'

Rodney didn't take any notice, but the woman next to Blanco did. 'Constable Blanco,' she said. 'Dana Reynolds, from *Nationwide*.'

The veteran reporter had managed to snag a spot right up the front. She was clinging to the fence with one manicured hand and holding an umbrella with the other. Her hair and make-up were somehow perfect despite the chaos.

'I know who you are,' Blanco snapped. 'The department has no comment.'

'Last time I checked, you weren't with the department anymore,' Reynolds said. 'They turned on you. Used you as a scapegoat, so they wouldn't have to take the blame for letting the criminal known as Viper infiltrate their department. Care to comment on that?'

She was trying to win Blanco over. It wouldn't work.

'Get lost,' Blanco said.

'I too have a source who can identify Viper,' Reynolds said.

That got Blanco's attention. 'Who?'

'You know I always protect my sources,' Reynolds said primly. 'You tell me who *your* witness is. Then I can tell you if my source is the same person. Because if it's not—if we have two independent sources—then the intel is more likely to be solid.'

'I don't trust you,' Blanco said.

Reynolds looked hurt, but Blanco was pretty sure she was faking it.

'Why do you think your witness is inside that building?' Reynolds asked. 'Is it because there are so many worried parents out here?'

Blanco's eyes narrowed. Witness 0 was a schoolkid. Reynolds was implying that her source was too. Could be just a lucky guess. Or . . .

'Does this sound familiar?' Reynolds asked. 'You receive an email. The sender says he knows who Viper is, but that it's only safe to reveal that information in person. Then he goes dark.'

'How do you know that?' Blanco was shocked.

'Same person, then.' Reynolds didn't look disappointed—in fact, she seemed relieved that only one person knew who Viper was. Maybe she had been worried about losing her scoop.

'How about this,' Blanco said. 'I'll give you his first initial. You give me his last initial. Then we'll know if we're talking about the same person.'

'Agreed,' Reynolds said.

'J.'

'D.'

Blanco sucked in a sharp breath through her teeth. They were talking about the same person. The message about Viper's identity had come from the email account of JARLI DURRAS.

NEVER TRUST A SNAKE

Anaconda *hated* basements.

Firstly, because the ceilings were so low. At two hundred and forty-five centimetres tall and with shoulders more than a metre across, Anaconda already struggled to fit through doorways and had to stoop in most rooms. Basements tended to be even more cramped, because the builders never wanted to dig too deep.

Secondly, because they were windowless. They reminded him of the prison cell where he had spent eight years for armed robbery. The guards and the other prisoners had made fun of him, making gorilla noises from behind the safety of the shatterproof glass. Someone had thought it would be hilarious to send him child-sized amenities—a tiny toothbrush, a tiny pillow, tiny shoes. They had guffawed, seeing the miniature objects in his gigantic hands.

They had all assumed he was stupid. In their minds, 'big' meant 'dumb'. But Anaconda was brilliant. He had memorised the angle of every surveillance camera, and the number of seconds it took each guard to get from one end of his patrol to the other and back. His hands may have been huge, but they were dextrous. When Viper mailed the set of lock-picks to Anaconda—cleverly hidden inside a child-sized laptop—he had already known how to use them.

Viper had told him to hurry out of the prison, but Anaconda hadn't. He had made several stops on his way. None of those creeps would ever mock him again.

Anaconda carried the jackhammer down the stairs with one hand, and dumped it behind the incinerator. Then he measured. Half a metre from the south wall, one point one metres from the east. This was the spot.

He was supposed to have done all this half an hour ago. His run-in with those kids had been an infuriating setback. If he found them again, he would tear them to pieces.

He plugged the jackhammer into the power point and thumbed the switch to start the motor. The steel wedge shuddered back and forth like an electric carving knife. If the concrete floor wasn't reinforced, he would break through to the tunnel below in about ten minutes. If it *was* reinforced, the task would take a little longer.

Anaconda balanced the jackhammer's chisel on the concrete and started digging. Most construction workers relied on the weight of the jackhammer to break up the concrete. Anaconda weighed almost two hundred kilograms—when he leaned on the handle, the blade sank right into the floor. Chips of concrete flew like ice. A TOXIC FOG of concrete dust rolled out under his feet. Sweat poured down his brow. No reinforcing steel. That was good. He would be out of here soon.

Clang! Clang! Clang! Anaconda quickly lifted the hot jackhammer off the floor. What was *that?*

It looked like metal, but not the kind used to reinforce concrete. It was a flat plate with a silvery sheen. The letter U was stamped in it, which was the chemical symbol for uranium.

Anaconda knew that uranium was highly radioactive. Exposure to it had damaged his pituitary gland as a child, causing him to grow to a spectacular size.

But judging by the colour, this was titanium. Either way, Anaconda wouldn't be able to drill through it. He chose another spot—one step to the right—and started the jackhammer again.

Before too long, there was another clang. Another metal plate. This time he could see the letter D.

Getting frustrated, Anaconda tried another spot.

Clang. Another. *Clang*. Soon he realised that the thick titanium plate covered the entire roof of the tunnel beneath, making it impossible to dig through. He and his colleagues were trapped here in the hospital, surrounded by police.

And there was a message stamped in the titanium plate.

Anaconda threw the jackhammer aside and screamed with rage.

BETRAYED

Something was happening outside. There was movement among the police. Bess pressed her face against the window, watching people collect equipment and strap armour onto their bodies. The crowd had been pushed back, further away from the temporary fence.

The police are coming in, Bess thought. *No! Not yet!*

If the cops waited five more minutes, the criminals would be gone, out through their secret tunnel. Bess didn't want the bad guys to escape. But if they were still here when the police broke in, she didn't think they would surrender peacefully. And then the hostages would get caught in the crossfire.

Bess started mouthing words at the police. *Don't come in yet! The bad guys are leaving! They're leaving!*

But it was dark out there, and still raining. Bess would be silhouetted by the fluorescent lights behind her. None of the police were close enough to read her lips. It didn't even look like anyone had noticed that she was trying to communicate.

She couldn't warn the police.

But she *could* warn the criminals.

A sick feeling formed in her guts, like a sea monster emerging from the deep. The criminals hadn't noticed the activity outside. If Bess told them that the police were about to come in, that might make them leave more quickly. The hostages would be less likely to get hurt.

Or the criminals might start preparing for the assault instead. A police officer might get shot with a crossbow bolt, or blown up by a grenade. And it would be Bess's fault. More blood on her hands.

Mr Hayes was distracted—he was whispering to another student. If Bess was going to warn the criminals about the impending invasion without him stopping her, now was the time.

She didn't. She decided to keep her mouth shut, and hope like crazy that no-one got hurt.

The jammer phone rang.

Bess jumped. The tension was killing her. In the reflection, she saw Taipan answer the phone.

'Anaconda,' he said. 'Have you made it through into the tunnel?'

There was a pause. As he listened, Taipan's face turned purple with anger.

'If you're lying to me . . .' he began. Bess didn't need to read his lips. Everyone in the room could hear him.

There was another pause.

'What?' Mamba demanded.

Taipan raised a hand, silencing her. Then he said, 'Fine. Go up to Theatre One. Kill Plowman. If Viper wants him alive, I want him dead. Let me know when it's done.'

Bess gasped. So did several other students.

Taipan ended the call. He was about to pocket the phone when Rattler grabbed him by the collar and slammed him against the wall. 'Are you crazy?' she snarled. 'If we betray Viper—'

'Viper betrayed *us,*' Taipan said. 'He's sealed up the tunnel with titanium plates. Anaconda can't dig through. We don't have a way out.'

'Why would Viper do that?' Mamba demanded.

'Anaconda said there was a message about Malburse. Maybe Viper knew one of the people who died there. This is his revenge.'

'That doesn't make sense,' Mamba said. 'If we get caught, the cops could use us to identify him.'

Taipan said nothing.

'Because you know his real name,' Mamba continued. 'Right?'

'No,' Taipan muttered.

'But you at least know what he looks like.' There was a warning tone in Mamba's voice. 'Because you told us you met him. *Remember?*'

Taipan was silent.

Mamba suddenly aimed her crossbow at Taipan's head. 'You sneaky, stupid little—'

'Hey!' Taipan raised his hands. 'How was I supposed to know Viper would do this? His jobs have always gone smoothly in the past.'

Rattler was aghast. 'You have us working for someone you've never even met?'

'You need me,' Taipan said. 'If you think you can face the police with a just a sword and a crossbow—'

'You're right,' Rattler said. 'We're much better off with a sword, a crossbow and an idiot.'

Bess had changed her mind. This was the perfect time for the police to attack, while the criminals were distracted.

Now, she mouthed at the window. *Come now*!

But once again, no-one saw.

'We can demand a vehicle in exchange for releasing most of the hostages,' Taipan said. 'We take one hostage with us so the police can't attack it on the way.'

'And drive where, genius? The police will just follow. They have helicopters.'

'You know me—I always have a plan B. Remember

the last job? The rocket Viper asked us to steal? I took two, and stashed the spare outside of town. Anything that follows us, we can shoot it out of the sky.'

Mr Hayes nudged Bess with his foot. 'Hey,' he muttered. 'Get ready to run. As fast as you can.'

'*What?* Where?' Bess whispered back.

'Follow the other kids, and the hospital staff. They're going to run through those double doors, deeper into the hospital. You'll probably be last through—don't wait for me. You can lock the doors from the other side, and trap the criminals in here. Then when the police come in, they can't use you guys as human shields.'

Bess didn't understand. 'But we'll never get past them!'

Hayes swallowed. 'I'm going to keep them busy.'

'How?'

'Just trust me.' Hayes stood up.

Mamba noticed first. 'Hey!' she snapped. 'Sit back down.'

The PE teacher cleared his throat. 'No.'

Mamba stormed over to him, crossbow raised. 'You picked a *really* bad time to make me mad,' she said. 'You have five seconds to get back on the ground.'

'It's my job to look after these kids,' Hayes said.

'I can't let you take any of them with you.'

'You seem to be forgetting who's boss around here.' Mamba moved closer, flanked by Taipan. At this range, she couldn't possibly miss. 'Five,' she said. 'Four. Three—'

'OK, OK.' Hayes bent over, like he was going to sit . . .

But then he lashed out with one of his lanky arms and grabbed the crossbow.

Mamba pulled the trigger. But the mechanism jammed, catching on Hayes's hand. Hayes grunted as the bow slapped his fingers. The crossbow bolt fell out instead of firing, jingling harmlessly to the floor. Then Hayes—still with the crossbow tangled around his hand—tackled Taipan.

As both men hit the ground, the other hostages all dashed towards the double doors. Bess wasn't the only one Hayes had warned. Everyone knew the plan.

Bess limped after them as quickly as she could. It was her worst nightmare—her life depended on staying with the group, and everyone else was too fast. She couldn't even keep up with the elderly patients. She was the fish right on the edge of the school, about to get swallowed by a shark. Doug wouldn't have left her behind. But Doug was gone.

Bess sneaked a glance back as she hobbled

towards the doors. Mamba and Taipan were both wrestling with Hayes, fighting for control of the crossbow.

But Rattler was chasing the kids instead. She knew that without hostages, there was no way to escape through the police cordon.

Rattler was fast. She ignored Bess completely, overtaking her and catching up to the other students with ease. Perhaps she didn't think Bess was a threat.

She was wrong.

Rattler raised her sword as she ran. It looked like she was going to slash at the knees of the screaming kids, stopping them from running away.

Bess swung one of her crutches at Rattler's ankles. *Thwack!* Rattler stumbled, but didn't fall. Her sword whipped harmlessly through the air.

Rattler whirled around to see Bess balanced on one crutch and holding the other like a baseball bat.

'Don't mess with me, kid,' she snarled.

'Don't mess with *me!*' Bess said, and swung the crutch at Rattler's head with all her strength.

Rattler expertly parried the blow aside. The leftover momentum nearly knocked Bess over. By the time she regained her balance, Rattler was driving the cutlass towards her face.

Bess raised her crutch. *Clang!* The impact sent SHOCKWAVES up her arm. She staggered backwards.

Rattler was already attacking again, this time stabbing at Bess's heart. It was even worse than when her parents made her try fencing. This time she had no mesh mask, or hard plastic bib.

Bess twisted aside. The sword missed her, but caught her shirt. The blade was so sharp that she didn't even feel the tug as it sliced through the fabric.

The rest of the students had escaped through the double doors, but it didn't look like they had locked them. *Come on, guys!* Bess thought. *Remember the plan!*

Rattler swung the blade sideways towards Bess's throat. Bess raised her crutch just in time. *Clang!* The collision took a chip out of her aluminium crutch. The cutlass looked unharmed.

Bess couldn't take much more of this. She had brought a crutch to a swordfight. If she didn't end this soon, she would end up skewered on that blade.

With a cry of rage, she raised both crutches, wobbling just on her legs. She swung her crutches inwards towards Rattler's skull, attacking from both sides. Rattler wouldn't be able to block both.

But just as the blow was about to connect, Bess felt a hand grab the back of her tattered shirt and pull. She lost her balance and tumbled over backwards. Her crutches swooped harmlessly through the air, and then she crashed to the floor on her back.

'Ow,' she groaned.

She found herself lying next to Hayes, who was facedown with Mamba's boot on his back, pinning him to the floor. Taipan stood on the other side—it must have been him who grabbed Bess.

The flesh around one of Hayes's eyes was swollen, and he had a split lip. 'That was brave,' he told Bess.

'You too,' Bess said, which didn't quite make sense, but she hoped he would know what she meant.

She heard the locks click in the double doors. At least the other kids had escaped.

GASLIGHTING

'Any progress?' Anya asked.

Jarli ground his teeth together. 'I've done about twenty centimetres.'

'We cannot climb through a ten-centimetre hole.'

'Oh, really? I'd better keep going then.'

It was maddening work. The laser scalpel melted the window as it cut through, so the two sides of the slice kept fusing back together. When Jarli had tried to wipe away the liquid glass with some tissues, they had simply burst into flames. If not for the hazmat suit, he would have been scorched. His new plan was to cut around the edges of the window, separating the glass from the metal frame. That seemed more effective, but it was taking way too long.

'I only have eighteen minutes of air left,' Anya said.

'Me too,' Jarli lied. Anya's phone didn't beep—maybe it couldn't hear him through the suit. The HUD on his visor said he had only ten minutes of air. Because of the heat, and the strain of holding up the heavy laser, he was using it up much faster than Anya.

He tried to focus on his breathing, slowing it down. His hands kept shaking. Was it just the effort of lifting the scalpel? Or was it the deadly botulism-H toxin taking hold, paralysing his muscles?

'Once we get outside,' Anya said, 'we still cannot take these suits off. That might expose others to the toxin.'

'The cops will have something airtight, right? They must. Like an oxygen tent or whatever.' *Or a body bag,* he thought. But it would have felt like jinxing themselves to say it out loud.

'There's a big oxygen tank outside. I saw it on the way in.'

'You think we can refill our suits once we're out there?' Jarli was doubtful. The big tank marked O_2 had been connected to the wall of the hospital by a narrow pipe, but he hadn't seen a tap or anything.

'Maybe we can do it in here.' Anya examined the wall next to Jarli. 'Look.'

Jarli glanced away from the laser for a second. Anya was pointing at something which looked like a power point. But the two outlets were round, and were marked OXYGEN and NITROUS OXIDE.

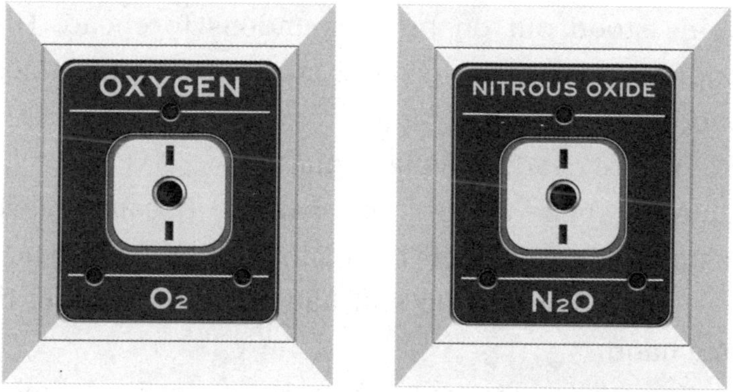

Jarli went back to cutting the glass. Thirty centimetres now.

'I don't know how to connect our air tanks to that,' he said. 'See if you can figure it out. But don't get the outlets mixed up. You don't want to fill your tank with laughing gas.'

Anya bent down to study the outlets. 'It looks—'

Smash! Something huge flew through the air and shattered against the wall, narrowly missing Jarli's head. Sharp tools rained down on the floor. Someone had picked up an operating table and thrown it at him!

'Found you!' a voice roared.

Jarli spun around in time to see Anaconda sprinting across the theatre towards him like a charging elephant.

Anaconda's face was twisted into a mask of rage. Veins stood out on his tremendous forehead. His boots slammed the ground so hard that the floor shook.

'You're dead!' the giant snarled.

And then things got worse. Because Jarli instinctively raised his hands to protect his face . . .

Forgetting that he still had the laser scalpel in one hand.

The laser sheared off part of Jarli's helmet, narrowly missing his ear. Cold air rushed into the suit and scorched plastic fell onto Jarli's hair, stinging his scalp. In a panic, he dropped the scalpel. As it fell, the laser beam carved a black line across the wall towards the gas outlets Anya had been examining—

Where it ignited the oxygen.

Just as Anaconda was about to crash into Jarli, flames gushed out of the outlet. A line of fire raced across the wall as the oxygen pipe ruptured, setting fire to the cladding in the wall.

Then the oxygen tank outside went up with a tremendous *KABLAM!* An explosion ripped out of the wall, and then the floor opened up to swallow Jarli and the whole world went a dazzling white.

Twenty seconds earlier

Bess squirmed under the weight of her own crutch. Taipan was leaning on it, crushing her ribs. She wondered if she could roll sideways, knocking him off balance.

Maybe. But she would still have Rattler's sword to deal with. And Mamba had reloaded her crossbow. Plus, Taipan had a flash grenade in his hand. He had removed the pin and was holding it closed manually. If the police shot him with their stun guns, Bess and Hayes would be blinded and scorched.

'We've lost the other hostages,' Taipan was saying.

'Doesn't matter,' Mamba said. 'With Anaconda, it'll be cramped in the escape vehicle. We'll only have room to take one hostage with us.'

'Which one?'

Hayes met Bess's gaze. Which one of them would be left behind?

'The girl is smaller, and easier to manage,' Mamba said. 'Kill the other one.'

Hayes squeezed his eyes shut.

'Wait!' Bess cried.

Ignoring her, Rattler raised the sword—

Then the world exploded.

Bess screamed as the ceiling disintegrated. Blocks

of masonry rained down, along with an avalanche of brick dust, an operating table, a laser scalpel, two people in space suits, and what looked like a *giant*—

But then Mamba fell on top of Bess, obscuring her view. Bess tried to push Mamba off, but already so much debris had landed on Mamba that Bess couldn't move her. She could hardly even breathe.

Boom! A secondary explosion shifted some of the rubble. Maybe it was Taipan's grenade. Broken glass rained down like wind chimes.

Soon the white flash of the explosion died away, leaving Bess in the DARK. She was buried alive. She only had the light between the cracks of the rubble to see by.

Mamba was still on top of her. She wasn't moving. She'd been struck by a spectacular number of rocks.

Help, Bess tried to scream. But there was no air in her lungs.

She was slowly suffocating in the blackness.

GOLIATH

'Move in, move in!' Detective Arno yelled.

The police swarmed up the hill towards the front of the hospital, where the entrance had been before the explosion. The front wall was just gone—it was like looking at an open doll's house. Ribbons of twisted steel and chunks of concrete were scattered all over the hillside. In a matter of seconds, the landscape had changed from a siege to a war-zone.

In her training, former Constable Blanco had seen photographs of bombed-out buildings. She had learned about the hazards of entering one—falling debris, toxic particles in the air, the risk of secondary blasts and fires. And those were just the hazards from a normal building. A hospital would be much worse, since half the debris could be contagious or radioactive. And four criminals were in there somewhere.

Just the same, Blanco ran up the hill alongside the other police officers. There was no time to be cautious. School kids and injured people were in there, including Jarli Durras and Kellin Plowman. She couldn't just stay back and wait.

In the chaos, no-one stopped her. Soon she was in the ruined foyer, climbing across the rubble like a mountain goat. She could hardly see anything through the smoke and dust. The other officers had goggles, masks, body armour and guns. Blanco was horribly vulnerable, with nothing except her civilian clothes.

Blanco coughed and rubbed dust from her eyes. In the torchlight she could see various objects scattered in the debris—half a computer monitor, a portable defibrillator shooting sparks, a chair with only one leg still attached. A reception bell was half embedded in one wall. Emergency lights flickered in the room above the collapsed ceiling, which looked like a surgical theatre. Something was on fire in the corner. No sign of the hostages, or the hostiles.

'Clear!' someone yelled.

Detective Arno was already headed towards the double doors on the other side of the room, which looked intact. 'Seal off the area,' she ordered. 'Johnson and Shu, go left around the building. Ruiz and Poe, go right. Don't let anybody leave. There are sixteen kids in here somewhere; their safety is—'

And then something huge erupted from the rubble.

Blanco jumped back as rocks tumbled. Arno screamed as a huge hand shot out of the debris and grabbed her. She was like a mouse caught in an eagle's claws. A giant emerged from the earth, illuminated by torches and emergency lights, his skin and his ragged clothes were grey with concrete dust. It was as though the rocks themselves had come to life. Blanco had never seen anything like it. She found herself frozen, her feet rooted to the rubble.

'Halt, or I'll shoot!' Rodney yelled from behind Blanco. The spell broke and she threw herself to the ground, to give him a clear shot at the giant.

The giant didn't halt. He raised Arno up with both hands and then threw her at Rodney.

Arno sailed through the air and crashed into Rodney. They both fell into a heap. Rodney's stun gun went flying.

The giant turned his furious gaze onto Blanco. Then he stomped towards her like a hungry T-Rex.

With no way of defending herself, Blanco turned to run, but she immediately tripped over an exposed pipe sticking out of the debris. She hit the ground and rolled sideways, trying to get out of the giant's path—

Then she bumped into the portable defibrillator.

Without even thinking, she grabbed the dented

paddles. As the giant reached for her, she rolled over and held up the paddles like a shield.

As soon as the giant touched the metal surface of the paddles, they kicked back in Blanco's hands. The giant bounced backwards as though he'd collided with an invisible wall. His whole body went stiff, and he hit the ground with such force that even more chunks fell out of the ruptured ceiling. He lay there, twitching.

Rodney was climbing to his feet, stunned. 'What . . . how . . .'

Blanco rubbed her face with trembling hands.

Arno was back up already, examining the fallen giant. 'We're gonna need to find some big handcuffs before he wakes up,' she said. 'I don't think zip ties will cut it.'

Something moved underneath Blanco. She lifted some of the broken bricks to reveal the back of someone's head. She shifted a few more, and saw someone else trapped under the first person. A girl.

'About time,' Bess wheezed. 'Get me out of here!'

Blanco dug frantically through the rubble, unearthing Bess and an unconscious woman holding a crossbow. *One of the criminals,* she guessed, signalling to Rodney to secure the woman and her weapon.

'Are you OK?' Blanco asked Bess.

Bess coughed and spat. 'You have to find Mr Hayes. He's under here somewhere. Hurry!'

Blanco kept digging. Arno and Rodney joined her. More police officers came to help with the search.

Soon they had uncovered several people, including the PE teacher, two kids in hazmat suits, and three more criminals. Two of the criminals were unconscious. The other—a squat man in swim goggles—was awake but said nothing. He just glared at everyone as Arno dragged him out of the rubble.

By some miracle, everyone was alive. The hazmat suits seemed to have protected the two kids who were closest to the explosion. The falling rubble had left some nasty scrapes and bruises on everyone else, but no-one had a broken skull. A police officer used a steel tube to break through the locked door to the corridor, where he found more than a dozen hostages—terrified, but unharmed.

'That's all four criminals,' Arno said, as she tightened some cuffs around the man's wrists. 'It's over.'

'There are five,' Bess said. 'Viper is here.'

Arno was at her side immediately. 'Did you say Viper?'

'He's upstairs, operating on Mr Plowman in Theatre One. You have to stop him!'

Arno grabbed Rodney and the police officer with the steel tube. 'This way,' she said. 'Come on!'

She ran through the double doors and disappeared.

The squat man in the handcuffs chuckled quietly.

'What's so funny?' Blanco demanded.

'You'll see.'

Arno sprinted up the corridor, flanked by two police officers. If Viper was here, then she had to get to that surgical theatre. Fast.

This was a chance not many police officers got. Arno had spent her whole career catching people who followed orders—killers-for-hire, thieves-for-hire, money launderers. Arno would arrest them and put them away, but someone else would immediately take their place in the criminal underworld.

Today she had the opportunity to make a real difference. To arrest the person *giving* the orders, not just the pawns who followed them.

Today, Arno would cut the head off the snake.

She hit the stairs and kept running. The route to the surgical theatres was branded into her memory. Years ago, she had waited outside one of them for hours while a BULLET was removed from her partner. A bullet paid for by Viper. Now it was time to get even.

An orange-haired paramedic was hovering in the corridor, his eyes wide. 'Thank goodness you're here,' he said. 'I've been hiding in the bathroom. Was that an explosion?'

'Get downstairs,' Arno hissed as she ran past him.

The doors were just ahead. Arno slowed down, not wanting Viper to hear her coming.

Because he was in there. He had to be. The building had been surrounded for hours. Even if he had finished operating on Plowman, there was no way he could have escaped.

She pressed her ear against the door. She could hear movement inside. The beeping of the heart monitor, the faint clack of metal on metal. The sounds of surgery. He was still in there.

Arno held up three fingers at the other cops. Then two. Then one. Then she clenched her fist.

One of the police officers rammed the steel tube against the door, right below the handle. The door crashed inwards and Arno stormed through, gun raised, adrenaline fizzing in her veins.

'Put your hands where I can see them!' she shouted . . .

At no-one.

Kellin Plowman lay on the operating table, unconscious. A surgical robot loomed over him, threading a short row of tiny stitches at the back of his scalp. The surgery was complete. No-one else was in the room.

'He can't have gone far,' she said. 'Search the building!'

As the other cops raced out of the room, Arno edged cautiously around the robot, her gun still up. A radio communications device—it looked like a modified signal jammer—was plugged into the control panel of the robot. The surgeon wasn't here. Someone had been controlling the robot remotely.

Arno grabbed Plowman's shoulder. He appeared to be waking up—his eyes were open now, at least.

'Where is Viper?' she demanded. 'Where did he go?'

Plowman smiled politely. 'I'm sorry—who is Viper?'

LONG HAUL

Everything hurt. Doug's back, neck and thighs had all cramped up. But he didn't dare shift his limbs. For all he knew, the drone was a hundred metres up, carrying the crate over a field of jagged rocks. The slightest movement might dislodge its grip, sending him tumbling to his death.

He didn't know how long he'd been in the crate. He couldn't reach his phone to check the time. After a while he'd started counting the seconds, but he'd given up at about five hundred. Wherever the drone was taking him, it was a long way from the hospital.

But that didn't mean he would be safe. It was the criminals who had put the crate on the rooftop. He could be going to their hideout.

A sick feeling in his guts told him that the drone was descending. He had nearly arrived.

Doug fought to keep still as the drone swerved several times. It felt like it was dodging trees, or swooping under power lines. He braced himself for impact, but was still shocked when it came. The crate hit the ground with a thud that crushed the foam packaging under his knees and forearms. The wooden floor of the crate left splinters in his palms.

There was a clanking sound as the drone detached. Then it whined away. Silence fell.

Doug listened for people or vehicles, but heard nothing. The drone must have dropped the crate off in a secret location, and the criminals would come to pick it up later. Doug needed to be gone by the time they got here.

He pushed the lid off, slowly, carefully, and poked his head out like a gopher.

The drone hadn't been taking him through trees—it had been taking him through doorways. The crate was indoors—it sat on an unsealed concrete floor between two walls made of temporary-looking plasterboard.

Doug climbed out of the box and turned around, increasingly confused. The two walls made a corridor with a T-intersection at each end. When he walked up and down the corridor, he realised that each branch of T-intersection led to another corridor with a T-intersection at each end.

He was in a maze.

The walls weren't much taller than Doug. They didn't reach the distant ceiling, which was insulated with a crumpled foil-like substance. The maze had been built inside a warehouse, or an aircraft hangar.

Maybe Doug could climb up onto the box and peer over the walls to find a way out. As he made his way back through the maze towards the box, he heard a faint voice.

'Victor Green. Nice to meet you.'

Then a different voice:

'Victor Green. Nice to meet you.'

Then the first voice again.

'Victor Green. Nice to meet you.'

The same line was repeated back and forth, two people saying the same words over and over, echoing around the warehouse so Doug had no idea where it was coming from. The first voice sounded like a recording, but the other was a little different each time. By the time he reached the crate, he was thoroughly unnerved.

A scuffle.

Doug quickly ducked behind the crate. He risked a peek, just as someone shuffled into view at one end of his corridor—a woman with a walking frame. At least, Doug thought she was a woman. She wore a shapeless hospital gown and her whole head was cocooned in bandages. All except for her eyes, which were concealed behind a pair of dark glasses—even though the corridor was already dark.

She was alone. The voices were coming from

somewhere else.

'Victor Green. Nice to meet you.'

'Victor Green. Nice to meet you.'

Despite the walking frame, Doug didn't get the sense from the woman's hands or bare feet that she was old. She clanked faintly as she walked. Doug saw steel pins protruding from her shins. Maybe she was recovering from an operation.

She didn't look like much of a threat. Doug stood up. 'Hey,' he whispered.

The woman froze. She turned to look at him, but didn't say anything.

'What is this place?' Doug asked.

The woman hobbled away as fast as she could.

Doug hovered near the crate, not sure whether to chase her. Then she was gone.

Whatever this place was, Doug wanted *out*. He scrambled up onto the crate and stood on tiptoes so he could see the layout of the maze.

It didn't take up the whole warehouse. Five or six turns would get him out. Most of the warehouse seemed to be occupied by a curtained-off area. Mysterious lights blinked behind plastic sheeting. At the other end of the warehouse was a big door for vehicles, and a small door for people. Both were closed, but maybe one would be unlocked.

'Victor Green. Nice to—'

The recording stopped abruptly. The sudden silence was unsettling.

Doug took one last glance at the route, and then jumped down off the crate. He ran through the maze towards the exit. Left. Right. Right—

Another scuffle.

Doug turned, expecting to see the woman with the walking frame again. But the corridor was empty. The sound had come from somewhere else.

He turned back—

And found someone standing right in front of him. He got a split-second view of a face covered in horrible burn scars before a gloved hand pressed a damp cloth over his eyes.

Doug tried to scream, but the cloth covered his mouth, too. Another gloved hand had grabbed the back of his skull so he couldn't move away. The cloth tasted like dishwasher detergent—it had a lemony sting.

He flailed at his attacker, but his arms felt suddenly weak and clumsy. His knees buckled. He hit the ground and his attacker knelt down next to him, keeping the cloth on his mouth.

'Shhhh,' Viper whispered.

Then Doug blacked out.

QUARANTINE

The time in quarantine was the longest two hours of Jarli's life.

He sat on a cold plastic bench in his undies, shivering, while three people in hazmat suits circled him with handheld microscopes, thermometers, Geiger counters and other devices he couldn't identify. Someone stuck a needle in his arm and siphoned some blood into a vial. Several times he asked about Bess, Anya, Doug, his other classmates and his family. The doctors—Jarli assumed they were doctors—said they didn't know anything.

The examination took place in a big tent, hastily erected on the lawn outside the hospital. The tent was inside another tent, which created a kind of airlock between Jarli and the outside world. A plastic tarpaulin covered the wet grass. The rain had started again, battering the canvas above Jarli's head.

Once they had completed their examinations, the doctors turned to leave.

'Where are you going?' Jarli asked. 'Am I infected?'

'We'll know more soon,' one of the doctors said. They all disappeared through the flaps.

Jarli sat there for a while, hugging his knees. Then he was too anxious to stay still, so he paced up and down the length of the tent.

What if I'm dying? he thought. *What if they don't let me see Mum and Dad? What if—*

He was interrupted when someone came into the tent. It was Constable Blanco, carrying a bundle of clothes—and not wearing a hazmat suit.

Jarli scrambled away from her, pressing himself into the corner of the tent. 'Get out!' he cried. 'I'm contagious!'

'You're not,' Blanco said. 'The disease control team say there's no sign of botulism H or any other pathogen in your system.'

Jarli sagged with relief. 'Really? Are you sure?'

'I'm sure.' Blanco tossed the clothes to him. 'Put these on, quickly. I don't have a lot of time. I'm not supposed to be in here.'

Jarli pulled his shirt on over his head, feeling the anxiousness unravel in his chest. 'The botulism box—the one in the hazardous materials room—was wide open,' he said. 'How could I not be infected?'

'I haven't seen the box you're talking about, but I overheard some hospital staff talking with the other police. Apparently there was supposed to be a vacuum flask *inside* the box—an extra layer of security. It's missing. Sounds like someone took it before you got there.'

Jarli hesitated, halfway through pulling his pants up. 'You think the bad guys stole it?'

'It's possible,' Blanco admitted.

'Why would Viper want a container of botulism H?'

'It's a worry, that's for sure. Who is he?'

Jarli was confused. 'Who?'

'Viper.'

'I don't know.'

Blanco stared at him. 'You sent me a message. You said you'd identified him.'

'No, I didn't.' Jarli was even more confused now.

'Are you messing with me?'

'Of course not!'

'Here. I'll show you.' Blanco pulled out her phone and brought up an email. She handed the phone to Jarli.

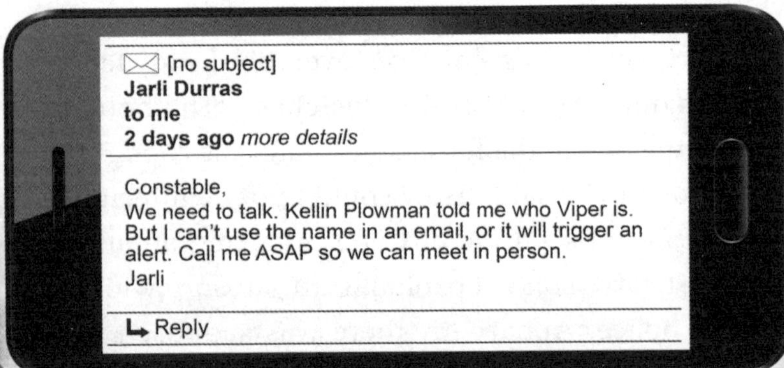

[no subject]
Jarli Durras
to me
2 days ago *more details*

Constable,
We need to talk. Kellin Plowman told me who Viper is. But I can't use the name in an email, or it will trigger an alert. Call me ASAP so we can meet in person.
Jarli

Reply

Jarli frowned at the screen. The message appeared to have come from his email address. But that could easily be faked.

'I didn't send this,' he said. 'Someone must have hacked my emails—or they could have spoofed my address using a PHP mail script.'

Blanco looked like she was about to say something else when Bess and Anya came in. Both were limping and covered in dust and sweat. But Bess was grinning from ear to ear.

'We did it!' she said. 'All the criminals are getting loaded into police cars outside!'

Even Anya was smiling. 'And I am not dying!' she said.

'Kelton: one,' Bess said. 'Bad guys: zero.'

Jarli hugged them both. 'I'm glad you're OK,' he said. He didn't mention the missing flask of botulism or the mysterious email—he didn't want to spoil the moment. And he was too exhausted to wonder what it might mean.

'Where's Doug?' he asked instead.

Bess's smile faded. Her chin dimpled like she was about to cry.

'What's wrong? Where is he?' Jarli asked again.

'He, uh . . .' Bess swallowed. 'He didn't make it.'

The shock almost knocked Jarli off his feet. '*What?* What happened?'

Bess explained about the underground prison, and the furnace, and the chimney. Jarli listened in growing horror. His friend had been burned alive.

'He might have . . . I mean, maybe he made it to the roof in time,' Jarli said, when Bess finished.

'I heard him screaming,' Bess choked. She looked like she wanted to say more, but she couldn't.

Jarli hugged her again, tears brimming over in his own eyes. Doug had been just a kid, like them. A decent kid, underneath his grouchy attitude. He'd risked his life to save Jarli's, several times. While working on Doug's robot they had become true friends, not that Jarli had ever said so. Now Doug was gone.

'The police haven't found his remains,' Blanco said.

'Meaning that he could have escaped?' Jarli said, clutching at straws.

Or that he burned away to nothing, said a gloomy voice in his head.

'If he survived,' Blanco said, 'we don't know where he is.'

Jarli wiped the tears on his sleeve. 'I want to go up there. To the roof.'

'Me too,' Bess said, sniffling.

Blanco shook her head. 'It's been searched. He's not there.'

'I don't care,' Jarli snapped. 'I have to see for myself.'

'We don't have time for this—'

'What about Plowman?' Anya interrupted. 'Is he alive?'

'Yes, believe it or not,' Blanco said. 'I wouldn't have thought someone could survive getting squashed in a car crusher and then getting amateur brain surgery, but it turns out that he's a tough nut.'

'Perhaps Viper is not an amateur,' Anya said.

'Well, he used a surgical robot—I don't know how much skill was required on his part. Maybe it's like using a self-driving car, or a robot vacuum. The machine has all the skill.'

Bess cleared her throat, but her voice still wobbled. 'I overheard the criminals talking. They said Viper had done it before.'

'Brain surgery?' Blanco stroked her chin. 'Now *that,*' she said, 'is interesting.'

'Why did Viper want to do surgery on Plowman in the first place?' Anya asked.

'OK, this is where things get weird,' Blanco said.

Jarli hung his head. *This* was where things got weird?

'I've been investigating privately. I think Plowman figured out Viper's identity,' Blanco continued. 'And he was smart enough to realise that this put him in terrible danger. So he added the information to Supply Chain.'

'Which is what, again?' Bess said.

'It's a string of encrypted data which can't be changed or deleted by anyone, ever,' Jarli said numbly. 'People use it for cryptocurrencies.'

'But it can also be used for recording other kinds of information,' Blanco said. 'Such as the names of criminal masterminds. Dana Reynolds has been digging too. She says Plowman changed his will. The new will stated that if Plowman died, his password would be made public. Everyone would be able to see everything he'd ever added to Supply Chain. And he adapted his pacemaker to broadcast his heart rate, so the will would be automatically activated as soon as his heart stopped.'

'So if Viper killed Plowman,' Jarli said slowly, 'then everyone would find out who Viper was.'

'Right. But Plowman's threat would only be effective if Viper knew about it. So he reached out to a couple of people. I thought you must have been one of them.'

'Why me?'

'He probably trusted you because of your app,' Blanco said. 'But his plan didn't work. Viper was too quick. He found out what Plowman knew before news about the will reached him, and got his men to put Plowman in a car crusher.'

'But that means we can see it.' Anya sounded eager. 'We can look at Supply Chain and find out who Viper is!'

But Jarli already knew what Blanco was about to say.

'No,' she said. 'It's encrypted and unhackable. We can't get to the data without Plowman's password.'

'But surely he will give it to you when he wakes up?' Anya said. 'He sounds like one of the good guys.'

'He's already awake,' said Blanco grimly. 'And he says he doesn't remember the password.'

Jarli was aghast. '*That's* what the brain surgery was for? To erase a password from his brain?'

'Not just the password,' Blanco said. 'All knowledge of Viper. He didn't even know what we were talking about. Viper couldn't kill Plowman, and couldn't threaten him, so he just removed himself from Plowman's mind.'

'Wow,' Anya said. 'That is brilliant. Evil, but brilliant.'

Jarli sat down on the bench. They were back to square one.

'Don't lose hope,' Blanco said. 'The police will retrace Plowman's movements over the last few weeks. Who he met, what he did. Maybe he'll remember something. Or maybe they'll find whatever evidence he found, and identify Viper independently. I wish they'd let me help.'

It did sound like a lot of work. Jarli sighed and rubbed his eyes. He was so tired.

'Do you think they'll let us take the rest of the week off school?' he asked.

Bess patted him on the back. 'Tomorrow's Saturday, buddy. Keep up.'

'Oh yeah.' He still couldn't remember Thursday.

Suddenly a strange feeling came over him. It was like the sense that he'd lost something important, but he wasn't sure what.

'Anya,' he said. 'This morning you said I'd sent you a message.'

Anya nodded. 'Have you remembered what it was about?'

'No. Can I see it? The message.'

'Sure.' Anya brought it up and handed her phone over.

I need to tell you about something. Find me tomorrow morning.

The text message appeared to be from Jarli's phone. Much harder to fake than an email address.

'I looked for you the next day,' Anya said. 'But

you were sick.'

'I don't remember being sick.' Baffled, Jarli ran his hands through his hair—

And then he felt them. Hidden in his hair, at the back of his scalp.

STITCHES.